LOVE DON'T LIVE HERE ANYMORE

Dangerous Love - Book Two

JOY BUSSU

Published by Blushing Books
An Imprint of
ABCD Graphics and Design, Inc.
A Virginia Corporation
977 Seminole Trail #233
Charlottesville, VA 22901

Joy Bussu
Love Don't Live Here Anymore

Print ISBN: 978-1-63954-083-9
v1

Prologue

Yolan Belle walked into the Ensemble Theatre for the premiere of '*Dream Girls*'; her yellow, custom-made Romeo Hunte form-fitting gown with the thigh-high slit caused her bronze-colored skin to glow.

She was turning heads as she walked, the liquid beading made it look as if it was melted and molded to her body like a second skin.

Her hair was perfectly coiffed, touched by the magical hands of Khyrs and Jaidyn who dropped everything to fit her in when she called.

Her manicured toes were wrapped in Ferragamo open-toed sandals from Shay and Monet's boutique that matched her gown perfectly, needless to say, she was perfection personified; her best friend and boss Tayana aka Whisper would be so proud.

As she reached the bar, she was the center of attention, men lifted their glasses to her behind their date's backs, eyebrows lifted in hopeful question, looking for an upgrade.

Yolan barely acknowledged them. One thing she hated more than anything else in the world was a whorish, cheating man and she made sure they knew it with her trademark deadly glare.

Her face lit up when she spotted his familiar tall frame at the back end of the bar, his back was to her as she moved his way. His custom gray suit hung from his 6'9", fit-thick frame highlighting his broad shoulders and muscular arms. At 5'2", Yolan had always been attracted to tall men, it was his height that first attracted her to Thomas 'Tower' White.

Yolan walked past him and slid onto the stool directly behind the pretty peanut butter hued female he was leaning in talking to, his perfect pretty boy smile on display as the woman reached up and stroked his face.

Yolan and Tower had been together for 2 years and 5 months and had lived together for almost as long. Imagine her surprise when he informed her he had a dinner meeting tonight, the same date and time she saw printed on the theatre tickets she had discovered in his suit jacket pocket a week ago when she went to drop off his clothes at the cleaners.

Yolan didn't trip or even ask a single question, instead she began to plan, and now she grinned with wicked excitement, as the last leg of her plan was about to go down.

She ordered an amaretto sour smiling sweetly at the bartender just as Tower looked past his pretty date and his eyes fell on her. She noted with pleasure as the color drained from his face, a look of fear dancing in his brown eyes.

She flashed him a cover girl smile and took a sip of the drink the bartender had just placed in front of her.

Thomas threw the rest of his drink to the back of his throat, moving his head when his date tried to touch his face again. He whispered something to his date and moved over to stand next to Yolan.

The woman, now feeling rejected, quickly rose from her seat in a huff glaring over at Yolan and Thomas and stormed off.

"Take it easy, Yo, she is just a business associate. There is nothing going on between us, I promise you," Tower explained running his hand over his bald fade haircut nervously.

Yolan smiled up at him as she continued to sip her drink. To think at some point, she was actually in love with this wayward dick ass joke of a man.

Not saying a word, she pulled a phone out of her clutch and after cueing up one of the videos it housed, she set it in front of him and pushed play.

Tower watched in horror as the video of him and his pretty date being a little too friendly played on the screen. They weren't having sex but they were damn close.

"Yeah, so that being said I'm going to need my keys. To the house and to the Bentley I bought you for your birthday," Yolan stated quietly smiling up at him again, relief washed over her as she said it. If she had to lie next to him one more night she might have killed him.

"Get the fuck outta here, you are really acting out, Yolan. Now if you want to go home and talk this shit out, cool, but nah, I ain't giving up the keys to anything for shit!" Tower growled quietly leaning on the bar signaling the bartender to bring him another drink before glaring at her.

Yolan finished her drink and stood up next to Tower, even in her stilettos she was barely past his waist.

"And here I thought this would be easy, pity." Yolan sighed and leaned on the bar looking up at him, shaking her head.

"Yeah, you got me all the way fucked up. I think you forgot who I am huh, Yolan?" Tower snapped, snatching his drink off the bar throwing it back, wincing when it hit the back of his throat.

"Correction, Tower, you have clearly forgotten who the fuck I am," Yolan said calmly as she slipped back onto the stool, crossing her legs. Her dress exposed her upper thigh and the yellow silk garter that cradled her all-white 357 'Angel'.

"I know you're crazy, Yo but you ain't crazy enough to shoot me in front of all these people. So yeah, go ahead and try to punk somebody else with all of that." Tower smirked, still clutching his empty drink glass rattling the ice around in it. "Now, like I said before, we can talk this all out at home where my shit is," Thomas said with steely determination, glaring down at Yolan. He stood upright to his full height so he towered over her. She smiled even brighter, this idiot was really feeling himself tonight!

"I have never been crazy, Tower, not in the least, but let me ask you this, did you forget who I run with or how deep we are willing to go to get results?" Yolan asked stirring her basically untouched drink with the straw in the glass. "Did you really think I wouldn't find out about your little double-cross you tried to blame on me?" Yolan asked, reaching over and cueing up a second video on the phone resting on the bar, this one of Thomas lying to save himself by throwing her under the bus about some missing money, the third and final video was him tonguing down his boss Bismark's wife, his hand down her shirt, his dick in her hand.

This was why they were here at this crossroad, not only had he been dumb enough to cheat and disrespectful enough to bring the bitches back to their house, he was also fucking his boss' wife, while stealing from him and lied on her about it!

She had no fucking clue until the day Bismark stepped into her office at Royalty Realty making idle threats in front of her clients about his missing money.

Yolan made a call to Tayana and Jazz who green-lighted her to handle the situation and was told to make them both disappear.

Thomas for disrespecting her and bringing trouble to her business and Bismark for overstepping his boundaries and going to Royalty in the first place. No one disrespected the crew and moreover no one fucked with business!

She was ordered to bide her time until moves were put in place to take down Bismark's entire operation with no man left standing. Thomas was the last man to fall because Yolan wanted to be there when it happened, you know since she 'loved' him and all.

Yolan watched with satisfaction as Thomas began to sweat, looking downright spooked before grabbing the phone and snapping it in two, his breath came out in panicked pants as he ran his hand down his face.

"What's done in the dark always comes to light, Tower. Now, for the last damn time before I really lose my patience, hand me my keys," Yolan said sweetly holding out her hand, her long lacquer painted nails glistened in the light that shined down from above the bar.

Tower reached in his pocket and dropped his keys in her outstretched palm.

Yolan dropped them in her purse, placed enough money on the bar to cover her tab as she moved to leave.

"Hold up, what about my stuff, Yo? And does Bismark know the truth about all of this?" he asked her cautiously, his face was covered in nervous sweat.

Yolan sighed, shaking her head like she hated to be the bearer of bad news.

"Why don't you ask him yourself? I'm sure he's *dying* to talk to you. As for your stuff, try the Salvation Army on Austin Street, I'm sure some of your stuff will still be there if you hurry," she said, smiling sweetly as flashing lights announced '*Dream Girls*' was about to begin.

Rini stepped up behind Tower, pressing her gun into his ribs. One of Jazz's security staff, a man they all called 'Pressure' fell in line on the opposite side of Thomas and nudged him in the opposite direction. Thomas cast one last regretful look over his shoulder at Yolan as he was escorted away.

Yolan paused long enough to make sure no one noticed them leaving out the back door that led to the alley and their 'work van' before sighing and walking towards the theater entrance.

Thomas' date, the woman from the car dealership he slipped his number to as Yolan sat in the manager's office signing the paperwork for his birthday present, a paid in full, black on black fully loaded Bentley stood next to the entrance of the VIP section of the theatre waiting on Yolan.

"Damn, Yo remind me never to piss you off," Meika said, shaking her head and taking the keys Yolan discreetly passed to her, the keys to Thomas' new Bentley.

It was already arranged that the car would be taken overseas, new VIN numbers and papers would be placed on it before it was resold at auction. It was a shame really, it was a beautiful car, for what was a beautiful man.

Right after he drove off in his new car, Meika, – an old neighborhood friend – who now worked for Joy and Rini at The Firm told her about him inviting her to their house to 'get to know each other a little better'.

After her visit from Bismark, Yolan sent Meika to plant more cameras in the house to see what Thomas was really up to. She was almost finished when Thomas came home early, so she slipped out of her clothes and was waiting for him in her bra and panties in the middle of the bed when he came into the room, pretending to be there waiting on him, telling him she wasn't afraid or worried about Yolan if he wasn't.

"This is not about being pissed off, Meika or even about him cheating on me, this was about business. Tower was getting greedy and he was getting sloppy, two things I have no time or respect for. If I was a dumb, clueless female, he would have fucked around and got a price put on both of our heads with that dumb shit he pulled and I ain't having it. Sometimes the one that holds you closest at night as you sleep is the very one sharpening the knife to drive into your back. Tower was just too stupid and cocky to notice my knife was bigger and sharper."

Chapter 1

"You sure you're all right, Yo?" Tayana asked Yolan two days later after the morning meeting. Her hand moved slowly down her baby bump as she looked over at Yolan with concern.

"You know me I am always good, Tay. Besides losing Tower ain't really a loss, erasing that man is most definitely a gain. I can honestly say I learned my lesson and will never be that stupid again," Yolan said, sitting back in her chair thinking to herself about how cute Tayana looked pregnant, she was actually glowing. "Anyway, on to more important things, how are you and my god baby doing? I'm surprised Jazz finally let you out of his sight," Yolan took the last bite of her spinach omelet, Ms. Lanie, Tayana's cook, had prepared for her. She had hung back after the meeting at Tayana's request.

Since finding out Tayana was pregnant, her husband Jazz had become more overprotective of her. This was the first time in a long time she saw Tayana alone at her own house – the one the crew held meetings at every morning – without Jazz in tow.

"We are both doing just fine and I had to tell his ass to back the fuck off before I killed him. I'm pregnant not dying and stop changing the subject. I know you, Yolan and you would have never let Tower move in unless you really loved him or at least thought you did.

I'm sorry he hurt you, Yo. I only wish it had been me and Mary Jane that sent his double-crossing ass to the hereafter. *No one* hurts my ladies, especially you, y'all are my sisters," Tayana said, her voice shaking as pregnancy hormones took over, trying to bring her to tears.

"I know, Tay but I was wrong, I made a mistake. A mistake, I know for damn sure, I will never make again, but I'm straight, you know how I get down. Now, before you go into the full-fledged emotional mode, anything else before I get to the office and my meeting with Mr. Feng?" Yolan asked, pulling out her mirror to make sure she had no spinach caught in her teeth and to check her makeup.

"Just one thing. Please, Yo, don't let this harden your heart, you are an incredible woman and one day the right man will come along and make sure you are treated like the queen you are," Tayana answered standing up from the table and moving closer to her.

"Okay, who are you and what have you done with Tayana? Those hormones got you tripping. I remember a time not too long ago you had washed your hands of ever falling in love and now look at your sappy emotional ass!" Yolan teased, allowing Tayana to pull her into a hug. She closed her eyes tight from the tears that wanted to fall.

She couldn't win for losing when it came to men and it was time for her to take her hat out of the ring for a while.

"I'm still here. Still Whisper, all fire and ice, but because of my best friend and the rest of my ladies pushing me to trust someone and allowing him to love me I'm more than that. I'm truly happy and I want that for all of you too," Tayana explained, letting Yolan go and watching her gather her briefcase and purse to leave.

"Tay, I am happy, trust me when I say that. But thanks for looking out for me. Now go find Jazz and hug and love on him for a while, some of us have work to do," Yolan teased, walking to the door that led to the foyer and the front door.

"*Xie Xie ni*," Yolan said 'thank you' in Mandarin, returning Mr. Feng's handshake and bow a few hours later.

Mr. Feng had a dual purpose for reaching out to Royalty Realty, he had large properties he wanted to purchase and 'antiques' he needed to move out of the country. Yolan's company was just the avenue he needed to do both.

"To you as well, Miss Belle. I look forward to moving forward with our business arrangement, please send the listings we discussed to my secretary as soon as you are able to," Mr. Feng said in English with a forced and obviously fake smile. The way his narrow eyes trailed up her frame before nodding approvingly told her all she needed to know about him. Mr. Feng had little to no respect for women and didn't particularly want to work with one, let alone an entire group of them. She figured he thought, like most men in power, women were only good for one thing, and he was only doing business with them because he wanted the best working with him which, he found out after lots of research, was their crew so he had no choice. Like Tayana said all the time, most people they conducted business with might not like what they were serving but, to have their needs met in the most professional way possible, they always ended up eating it anyway.

"I will compile the listings and have them sent over before the end of the day," Yolan answered, looking over her shoulder when the bell above the door chimed alerting her that someone had walked into the office.

She watched as her business partner Asia aka Neutral greeted the tall, suit-wearing gentleman and began to engage him in conversation.

Asia was yet another childhood friend of hers and Tayana's, she was not in the crew but was trusted and protected like she was. She, like Tayana, was having her first child, they were about a month apart in gestation.

"As for your antiques, I will have my associates get in touch with you to make the necessary arrangements in a few hours as well," Yolan stated, moving to escort Mr. Feng to the door.

"Perfect, I will await your associate's call, until next time, take care Miss Belle, *Zai Jian*," Mr. Feng stated pausing his exit again to shake Yolan's hand.

"*Zai Jian* – Goodbye in Mandarin – Mr. Feng and thank you in advance for your business, I guarantee you won't be disappointed," Yolan said smiling as she shook his hand before watching him leave.

The $2,000,000 he wanted to have cleaned and transported once a month through their channels would be a great addition to the crew's bottom line and reputation.

Yolan turned to move back towards her office when she felt eyes watching her, the tall gentleman sitting with Asia was sipping coffee looking over at her curiously.

"Yolan, this gentleman is interested in purchasing property on Caroline Street in the Museum District," Asia explained, gesturing to the still silent gentleman, his intense gaze was still trained on Yolan as he continued to drink his coffee.

Yolan could tell from how his long legs were bent in front of him, his knees inches away from touching the underside of Asia's desk that he was at least 6'6".

His beige, tailored Armani suit complemented his milk chocolate hued skin, his big hand dwarfed the coffee cup he was gripping, just that quick glance of him had a few wayward thoughts popping up in her head.

"Ah, perfect, great location. We have a few units that just came up on the market, do you know in which building you would like to purchase Mr.–?" Yolan asked, settling in the second chair positioned in front of Asia's desk while admonishing her hormones as she crossed her legs facing him.

"Devoe, Ryan Devoe and to answer your question, I am looking to purchase one of the buildings as a whole, not just a few units, is that something your company can handle or do I need to take my business elsewhere?" he asked, turning his body in his chair to full-on face Yolan with a small business-like smile on his face.

Yolan smiled at his no-nonsense air and at his handsome face. Sometimes she swore God had a serious sense of humor when it came to her, 'tall, dark and handsome' like the man sitting beside her wasn't just her type, it was her kryptonite!

He had a smooth, somewhat angular face, his honey-brown eyes were shielded by full eyebrows, his nose was a nod to his ancestors, full and proud. His soft-looking full lips peeked out from the well-groomed, full beard that hugged his face.

"I assure you, Mr. Devoe, we can handle whatever you choose to throw at us. Now I know there are three new buildings going up in that area, the starting bid for the cheapest building is over $300,000,000. Should I have Asia pull those up for you?" Yolan asked, standing and going to pour herself a cup of the gourmet coffee he was enjoying.

"With all due respect, Yolan, is it? I would much rather work directly with you on this. While I'm sure Asia is capable in most instances, I need the experience of an expert on this," Ryan stated, standing and joining her at the coffee station.

Yolan felt her ears grow hot in anger at the disrespect he

threw at Asia. Like everyone else in their crew, she only worked with the best of the best.

"Mr. Devoe, I assure you if we chose to work with you, you would be well taken care of by our entire team including Asia, who is, by far, one of my best agents as well as my business partner. That is how it works here at Royalty.

If that does not appeal to you then maybe you *should* take your business elsewhere as you previously alluded to," Yolan stated, calmly bringing her cup to her lips, blowing on it to cool the steaming coffee before taking a cautious sip.

Ryan's eyes darkened as he watched her, before pouring more coffee into his own cup. Almost defiantly he took a healthy gulp of the scalding hot coffee, while looking at her pointedly.

"I see. Perhaps, I should consider that while I am reaching out to one of your competitors, to assure that my needs are met?" he challenged with his eyebrows arched looking at her from behind his raised coffee cup.

Yolan moved closer to Asia and set her coffee cup on the corner of her desk, her hand rested on the back of Asia's high back chair.

"Perhaps you should, and when you come to realize that *no one* in the greater Houston area will give you the service we will here, at Royalty Realty, with our attention to detail and top notch services, you will be back. The accolades and awards hanging on the walls in this room are not just for show, we worked hard for each one and earned our reputation." Yolan picked up her coffee and took another sip. "Now as enlightening as it has been to speak with you today, Mr. Devoe, we do have work to do. I'm sure you don't need me or Asia to show you to the door," Yolan stated, her smile not quite reaching her eyes.

Ryan took his time finishing his cup of coffee before gathering his trench coat and briefcase.

"Ladies, it's been a pleasure, thank you for the coffee. I have to admit, when I walked in and heard you speak Mandarin, I had high hopes of this establishment having what I was looking for," he said looking over at Yolan, returning the half-hearted smile she tossed at him.

"As I said before, Mr. Devoe, shop around, see what's out there and make an appointment with us when you are ready to come back. I will set aside a few listings for us to discuss if and when you are willing to respect me *and* my team. Until then take care, Mr. Devoe," Yolan replied confidently and turned, moving back to her office.

She settled behind her own desk and logged in to get the listings Mr. Feng would be interested in, when she heard the bell at the front door sound before their heavy oak door snapped closed as Ryan Devoe left.

She closed her eyes to check her attitude. Men, especially cocky ones like him, got on her fucking nerves, or at least that's the lie she was telling herself at the moment, as the soft touch of feathery, light tingles moved up her spine just replaying how good he looked in that suit!

Ryan folded his long legs into his custom painted, mother of pearl colored Bentley Continental GT, his right eye twitching, something that always happened when he was aggravated. He was given an assignment and he needed the right people on board to make it happen. He didn't have time for bumps in the road like the one he just got from Yolan Belle.

Like just who the hell did she think she was? Women didn't talk to him or dismiss him the way she did. The fact she didn't even bat an eyelash when he said he was going to competing realtors really resonated deep with him. It told him either she was a very foolish businesswoman who let her wounded pride get in the way of a multi-million dollar deal or, just as she said, she and her team were the best of the best so they could take or leave his business and it didn't affect them either way.

More than anything else it was the very last thought crossing his mind that was annoying the fuck out of him. From the minute she sat next to him at Asia's desk, with that sexy ass smile of hers, he wanted to know more about her, not Royalty, but her as an individual. Even though she and her strong personality were the opposite of everything he was usually attracted to.

For now, he was going to let her think she had the upper hand and had even thrown him off of his game a bit, but he knew better. He would do some research and make sure Royalty really was the powerhouse she made them out to be and, even if they weren't, he was coming back for many reasons. The first, of course, was to satisfy his own curiosity and try to figure out what it was about Yolan Belle that had him ready to stake his claim after their very short encounter.

Chapter 2

"My understanding was we would be collecting payment in full on the 15th, Freeze. According to the Boss Lady we still have not been paid. Care to explain?" Yolan asked, smiling coldly at one of their newest runners over dinner several weeks later.

Jazz hired Freeze and his crew because no one in his businesses or even Whisper's worked directly in the drug trade anymore. But they had clients who still needed trusted connections in that regard, so the up and coming crew was given the opportunity to move up from their minuscule hand to mouth operation and make some real money with a real team.

It was sad they didn't take working with Jazz and Tayana as seriously as they should have and now they were late paying the percentage owed to 'Jazz and company'. After a month and a half of them lying, ducking and dodging the powers that be, Jazz and Whisper called up the ladies to do what they did best.

Yolan decided the best way to address the situation was to invite herself to their weekly business dinner to collect the money and send a warning. The meeting was set in the private back room of the restaurant 'Sweet's'.

With Tayana being pregnant, Yolan was doing a lot more footwork than usual, not that she minded, keeping busy kept her happy.

Rini, Joy, along with Shay and Monet were seated at the table with her.

Each one of them sat next to one of the four boys in his crew.

Pressure and Pain from Jazz's crew were seated nearby as well.

"Yolan, I know Jazz didn't send you and your *girl* crew to collect for him!" Freeze chuckled, taking a swig of his beer. "Y'all supposed to have more sense than to blow up into my spot, in my hood, while I am trying to enjoy my muthafucking meal and conducting business. You bitches got a death wish or something?" Freeze asked, sitting back showing Yolan he was packing.

His four boys followed suit, grinning, sucking their teeth, gold and platinum shining.

They were so cliche, spending all their money on grills, chains, and flashy cars, it was a miracle they hadn't all been arrested yet. The females at the local strip clubs and VIP's bottle service stayed paid because of these idiots burning through every dollar they made as quickly as they made it.

"Funny, Freeze, I was about to ask you the same question," Yolan said deadly serious, placing an iPad on the table.

She and the ladies all cocked their guns under the table-cloth in rapid succession.

Freeze was new to the area, so Jazz had tried to be patient, give him the benefit of the doubt but Freeze was also young and didn't know who he was dealing with. It was unfortunate that some lessons learned were hard ones but once learned, they were never forgotten.

"You owed us $450,000 on the 15th of October and, seeing how you decided to play this cat and mouse game with us, that price is now $550,000 due immediately." Yolan lifted her right leg, propping her foot between Freeze's legs on his chair, her leg hid Angel from view.

"Yeah, you bitches is straight tripping. I don't give a *fuck* about you and your weak-ass girl crew or the little pea shooters y'all working with, so I strongly suggest you remove your fucking foot from my chair unless you are showing me a preview of the pussy you about to give me," Freeze snapped, gripping his dick and sucking his teeth, glaring over at Yolan.

Yolan sighed and dropped her smile and pressed her foot forward, catching Freeze's balls between her foot and the chair.

She shifted towards Freeze and leaned further forward replacing her foot with Angel.

To any onlooker, it looked like she was moving in closer, getting a little friendly.

His smug face changed as he caught on quickly, Yolan pressed Angel deeper into his crotch.

"That is the last time you will refer to me or anyone in my crew as 'bitches or girls' do you understand me? And, sweetie, that little meat you packing? I've seen bigger in a box of brown and serve breakfast sausages, so miss me with all that bravado. Now, unless you want to carry your balls out of here in a to-go box, I strongly suggest you pay what you owe. Oh, and one more little tidbit, this restaurant? You know the one you called your spot? In your hood? Is 100% owned and operated by our crew so please make a scene because Angel here has a hymn she is dying to sing tonight," Yolan said softly, pressing her gun so deep into his scrotum it brought tears of pain to his eyes.

She knew for a fact that all the ladies had their guns

pressed in various body parts of his crew, sweat gathered between furrowed brows and foreheads all around the table.

Freeze glared at her while he took his phone out of his pocket and grudgingly but quickly transferred payment to an offshore account set up for their transactions. Yolan smiled as the iPad pinged, an alert popping up confirming payment.

"Well, now wasn't that easy? You have an outstanding balance at the gallery as well, correct? $200,000, I believe? You have until midnight tomorrow to pay it and once that payment is received that concludes your business in Texas for good. Might I suggest Colorado as a new base of operation, perhaps New Mexico even? We will give you a week to make that move," she stated, smiling sweetly. Angel was still resting between his legs making sure he understood her meaning.

Freeze rolled his eyes at Yolan, sucking his teeth in anger. "Man, you tripping, strong-arming me and shit! How the fuck am I supposed to pay your crew and relocate all in a fucking week? This is some bullshit!" he hissed, glaring over at her.

"Sounds like a personal problem. You should have planned ahead instead of popping bottles in VIP. Pawn your grill, perhaps?" Yolan offered and stood up after concealing Angel, smiling at Freeze.

If looks could kill she would have been six-feet under.

"And what if we refuse?" Freeze asked, pressing his luck. He would be damned before he let a crew of mostly women he should be dicking down, run him out of town! He wasn't a fucking pussy!

Pressure and Pain moved up behind him and *helped* him to his feet. The ladies all remained seated, guns still ready to sing.

"Then I guess alternative plans will be made for you and your crew and we welcome the task of assisting you in your *relocation*," Yolan stated putting her Michael Kors bag on her shoulder. She signaled for the manager, another one of their security team they gained from Jazz named 'Goon'.

He moved swiftly in the room and closed the heavy, sound-proof door as he entered.

"Can you inform Teddy the restaurant needs to close early tonight? It appears we have a leak in the boiler room," Yolan stated looking pointedly at Freeze.

Goon pulled out his phone and relayed the message immediately.

The shuffle of people being moved towards the exit could be heard a few minutes later.

"Man, fuck you and this town! Tell Jazz and Whisper they can eat a dick!" Freeze snapped, gripping his tiny package again.

Any other comments were silenced by a series of blows to his abdomen by Pain. Yolan watched all of Freeze's crew stand up and move away from the table and Freeze.

"Ay, Yo, he don't speak for all of us, you want us to disappear, we disappear," Freeze's second in command, Blue started reasoning with Yolan and the rest of the crew.

"Man, fuck you, Blue, bitch ass coward! How are you going to let some wannabe gangsta bitches scare you?" Freeze shouted spitting blood on the floor, Yolan was sure that Pain's punches had ruptured something.

The remainder of his crew, and Yo and the ladies, watched as he was dragged from the room towards the boiler room still cussing, mainly at Yolan and Blue.

"Freeze, I kept telling your stupid ass not to play around with Jazz and Whisper but you wouldn't listen!" Blue shouted after him, no shame whatsoever that he switched loyalties so fast.

Yolan watched as Blue pulled out his phone and pressed a few buttons, about fifteen seconds later the iPad in her bag pinged.

Blue settled the crew's debt and looked expectantly at Yolan.

"We cool?" Blue asked, still gripping his phone, his hands folded in front of him.

"Disappear," Yolan answered coldly and moved from the door to let them all pass, they all walked out quickly and silently.

"Consider us gone, Yo," Blue called over his shoulder as they left.

"Are we going to let them live, Yolan?" Joy asked tucking her gun back into her waistband at the small of her back.

Joy didn't have cute names for her guns, she just handled them with precision and expertise. Joy was the bookworm of the crew, she read books on everything but her favorites were on war and weapons.

"Watch 'em, I'll make the call to see what Jazz wants to do since he brought them to us. Honestly, I see where Blue was coming from but his actions do have me questioning his character, and obviously his loyalty to his boy. Keep your phone on, I'll let you know," Yolan said as she pulled out her phone and sent a text to the valet to have her car out front, she threw them a smile over her shoulder as she dialed Jazz's number to let him and Tayana know what just went down.

"Yolan?" A deep voice called her name from behind her, not just any voice either, it was the voice of Ryan Devoe.

Yolan groaned inwardly as the butterflies in her stomach took flight immediately. Despite the fact, the investment banker had rubbed her the wrong way by insulting Asia, implying he could get better service elsewhere and by just being an arrogant ass when he couldn't have his way, his handsome face and sexy, deep voice had found their way into her memory bank and sometimes even her dreams causing her to wake up all out of sorts the following day.

"Yes?" Yolan finished her call with Jazz and sent a message to Joy with his instructions: *'Make sure the relocation to the new house goes smoothly, the moving van should be pulling off tomorrow afternoon at the latest and make sure to confirm that they arrive safely, they have a habit of getting lost.'*

Translation: Watch them, make sure they leave by tomorrow afternoon at the latest and make sure we know where they land so we can continue to watch them because slippery, disloyal people like them cannot be trusted.

"I'm sure you don't remember me, my name is Ryan Devoe, we spoke briefly in your office about my company wanting to purchase a high-rise in the museum district," he stated, looking down at her, his hand lightly touched his beard before he put it in his pocket and licked his lips.

Nervous. He was nervous. That was the first thing Yolan picked up on. His reluctance was the second, he didn't like having to come back to her, that would mean having to admit he was wrong, something she could tell he didn't do often.

She thanked and tipped the valet and walked over to her open driver's side door.

"On the contrary, I remember you quite well, Mr. Devoe, I never forget a face or a voice. That being said, call the office in the morning, we can schedule an appointment to go over the properties in the area I set aside for you. Have a good night," Yolan said, right before she slipped behind the wheel of her silver Jaguar XJS and pulled off.

She smiled knowingly as she gazed at Ryan in her rearview mirror, trying her best to ignore how excited she already was at the thought of seeing him again.

Ryan bit the inside of his cheek as he watched her car pull off, he hated the fact she had been right, everywhere he went and everyone he spoke to regarding his endeavor told him the same thing, the team at Royalty Realty was the best place for his needs, it still tripped him out that not one business or person had a bad thing to say about them.

The other thing bothering him at the moment was he hated the fact that she looked even better tonight than she did the first time he saw her, her arrogance and no nonsense demeanor continued to pique his interest. Once again he was reminded of the fact that those personality traits would normally be a red flag or a warning that she was not the type of woman he wanted to be involved with. But no matter how many times he had tried to talk himself out of his growing interest in her and keeping things professional, his body would take over the conversation and tell him otherwise.

"Hey, Yolan, Mr. Devoe is here for his appointment, do you want to meet him in the conference room or here in your office?" Asia asked peeking her head in Yolan's office about a week later. After an hour of back and forth with Asia it was decided she would take the lead with Mr. Devoe after all.

"Leave him in the lobby for a few, he's really early. I will be out in a moment, I have a few things to finish up first," Yolan answered, not bothering to look up from her computer, compiling some new listings that had just become available.

"Okay, I will let him know to get comfortable," Asia answered with a smirk.

She had worked with Yolan for over ten years, was friends with her for fifteen before that and knew something about Ryan Devoe rattled the hell out of Yolan's cage and whatever that something was it was exactly what Yolan needed.

That's why she argued her down about him, yeah she

could take the lead and prove to him she was more than capable of assisting him but why would she do that?

It was obvious he already knew that or he wouldn't be back in the office, sitting in the lobby ready to talk business, besides if she was sure of anything it was that Yolan was the one who needed to work with him for her own damn good.

Yolan loaded all the listings to a jpeg folder and spent the next twenty minutes finishing up some last minute details on Mr. Feng's deal. After sending the contracts for Mr. Feng to review, she stood, took a deep breath and adjusted her favorite cream Vera Wang skirt and pulled Angel from under her lavender sleeveless silk blouse at the small of her back and placed the gun in her middle desk drawer.

Ryan Devoe was not a threat so her 'girl' was not needed.

After pulling the actual paper files of the properties she had researched and adding the new ones, she stepped out of her office to start her meeting with Ryan Devoe.

"We have our coffee imported from Kenya, that's why it tastes so good. I told Yolan sometimes I think that's the main reason we have so many return clients," Asia explained, laughing a little as she handed Ryan a cup of coffee.

Yolan smiled at how cute she looked in her maternity top and slacks and ballet slippers, she couldn't wait to be a god mommy to her and Tayana's babies!

"Good afternoon, Mr. Devoe, I apologize for the wait. Would you like to join me in the conference room?" Yolan asked walking up to Ryan, extending her hand for him to shake.

His massive soft hand wrapped around her small one taking the chill out of the air-conditioned office instantly. Their eyes met briefly as she pulled her hand away.

Today he was dressed a little more casually in charcoal gray slacks, a simple but tailored and professionally pressed button-down and tie, no suit jacket, he wore wire-rimmed glasses that brought more attention to his handsome face.

"Yolan, you can call me Ryan and there was hardly any wait. I know I was quite early, I usually am. Before we begin I must say you were correct, after several weeks of research and recommendations all paths led back to you and Royal Realty," Ryan stated, looking slightly uncomfortable at the admission.

"I see. Well, in any case, we are glad you decided to give us a chance, follow me, please?" Yolan turned quickly to hide her knowing smirk and led him to the conference room. Like she told him before, they were the best, tried and true, and now he knew it wasn't just talk on her part.

He settled in a seat in front of the monitor mounted to the wall in the corner of the conference room as she cued it up, it was wireless linked to her laptop.

"So, Mr.– I mean, Ryan, I have found six properties in the museum district that might appeal to you since our last conversation. One thing we failed to discuss was the number of units so I made sure to include options on units as well," Yolan stated and handed him the hard copies she had been carrying.

She noticed out of the corner of her eye, as she leaned over to grab the remote to start the slideshow, Ryan's eyes slowly moved up her body stopping on her ample heart shaped ass. Several seconds passed as he studied her.

"Ryan? Shall we get started?" Yolan asked her eyes narrowing as he refocused his gaze to the folder in front of him, clearing his throat, loosening his tie and blushing slightly.

Yolan clicked on the first slide and their meeting began.

"Yolan I must say you are very thorough, you even answered questions I never would have thought to ask. I am truly impressed," Ryan said, placing the folder with his notes scribbled on them in his briefcase.

"Thank you, Ryan, as I said before we aim to please, our attention to detail is our claim to fame. I will begin to make arrangements for you to see the properties once you check your schedule and give me the dates and times you are available," Yolan answered, noting again how he took the liberty to look her up and down slowly. He was getting on her damn nerves with that shit, or at least that was what she tried to convince herself was the reason for the amount of restless energy moving through her body at the moment.

Several times during their two-hour meeting she noticed his eyes roaming over her body or face, so much so, she would have to point something out about a particular amenity or feature of a property to get him back on task. Just the thought that a man like Ryan could be attracted to her as well, was doing a number on her psyche. Even as her common sense kept telling her to not even begin to think about him in any other way because it would not end well and she knew it.

"Yolan, as I told you before I'm ready to buy this property, my funding is already lined up and good to go. So you can immediately begin scheduling the showings, and I will make myself available for them," Ryan informed her matter of factly, subjecting her to yet another lustful glance. "I'm curious, will you be at the showings or will it be Asia?" he asked, standing up from the table, his hand in his pocket.

Yolan powered off the 52" monitor and grabbed her water bottle from the table before looking over at him.

"Does it really matter if the end result is the same?" Yolan asked, staring him down, she needed to get and keep her head out of the clouds.

Yeah, he had a cute thing happening, honestly he was fine as hell. But she, like most of the crew, was careful not to mix business with pleasure and this strait-laced, by the book man standing in front of her, just wasn't what she needed in her life.

His eyes narrowed slightly as he licked his lips, staring into her eyes. "I suppose it doesn't but I have to say I have rather enjoyed working with you this afternoon, I like how your mind works, you get me," he said with a small smile.

"Well, considering the fact you haven't seen Asia in action yet you might change your mind," Yolan challenged, taking a quenching drink from her water bottle. He and those eyes had her almost ready to change her stance, Lord give her strength! "However, you will be meeting me for showings, it's getting a bit too uncomfortable for Asia to be on her feet for hours on end," Yolan informed him, walking to the door of the conference room which he reached around her to open.

"Good to know, and, for the record, I admire the loyalty you all have here. A lot of places? Partner be damned, they would have cut each other off at the knees to collect a commission of this size," Ryan said as he followed her back down the hall.

She looked over her shoulder and caught him staring at her ass again. His bottom lip caught between his teeth.

"Another reason why we are the best, loyalty trumps money every time. When we close this deal with you, it's a win for the entire team, not just the individual. We are all putting in the work for our clients so we all reap the rewards, period. It took a long time to get a team like this but I am grateful for them all," Yolan answered giving him a look that let him know she knew what he was doing.

When they made it back to the main lobby, Asia wasn't at her desk, since the door was still unlocked Yolan assumed she was in the restroom.

"Well again, Yolan it's been a pleasure and I look forward to seeing the properties as soon as possible. I had my secretary send over all the necessary paperwork so if I see something I like we can bid right away," Ryan stated reaching out to shake Yolan's hand.

She shook his hand and he held hers a bit too long while smiling down at her, his bottom lip caught between his teeth. Tayana chose that exact moment to walk in the door.

Her eyes bounced instantly from Yolan to Ryan to their hands. Her face lit up and spread into a huge smile, her eyes suddenly dancing with mischief.

"Hey, Yolan, I know I'm a bit early for our meeting so if you don't mind I will make myself comfortable in your office while you finish up?" Tayana suggested not waiting for her to answer as she headed in that direction.

"Sure, Tay, we were just finishing up anyway," Yolan called out after her, pulling her hand from Ryan's.

"Your sister?" Ryan asked, watching Tayana leave the lobby, her pregnant belly leading the way.

"Pretty much, anyway if there is nothing else, I will contact your secretary with the showing dates and times?" Yolan asked, moving back a few steps.

"No, the card I gave you has my information on it, you can call me directly," Ryan insisted, his hand on the door handle.

He nodded and smiled in Asia's direction as she came back through the lobby and sat at her desk.

"Good to see you again, Asia. I will speak with you soon, Yolan." He smiled down at her again opening the door to leave.

"Sounds like a plan and talk to you soon, Ryan." Yolan watched him leave and let out a shuddering sigh, she turned and was face to face with the two preggos who were looking over at her with knowing grins.

Asia from her high back chair and Tayana leaning on the door frame of the small walkway that led to Yolan's office.

"So, I take it the meeting was a success?" Asia asked

feigning innocence, playing with the rubber band ball from her desk.

"If you must know, yes, it was, Asia, the commission from this sale will be one of our biggest ever," Yolan declared, ignoring Tayana and her know-it-all ass altogether.

"Everything about Ryan Devoe is big, so a big commission seems fitting. But I'm sure I don't have to tell you that do I, Yolan?" Asia teased looking over at Tayana cracking up laughing.

"Neutral, that is the first thing I noticed too! I was just about to ask, did you see the size of that man's feet and those hands? Whew, honey!" Tayana said laughing loudly, fanning herself and sitting in one of the chairs in front of Asia's desk.

Yolan glared at both of them, she had noticed that and more. His honey brown eyes, those soft looking lips, and that sexy ass slow smile had her checking herself while she was checking him several times during their meeting.

"He is a client, a straight and narrow client at that, so yeah, no," she snapped walking back to her office, trying to erase the vision of the last slow drag his eyes did up her frame.

"Okay, keep telling yourself that, Yo! That's why you wore that 'cheeks ahoy' skirt of yours, huh?" Tayana called out to her retreating back.

Yolan came back out to Asia's desk. "Whatever, Tay! I wore this skirt because it's one of my favorites, a gift from you I might add, and it makes me feel pretty," Yolan argued blushing.

"Yo, please! All that might be true, but we both know that ass-hugging skirt turns heads, and today, that tall ass Mr. Man who was here, when I got here, is the head you were intent on turning," Tayana said laughing, running her hand down her swollen belly.

"Yeah all that boisterousness is disturbing my godchild, so chill all the way out please," Yolan snapped sitting in the other chair, placing her hand on Tayana's stomach where the baby instantly kicked. She smiled because her god baby loved her already.

"Seriously though, Yo, you should give the man a chance. You know he wants one," Asia said, shaking her head trying to reason with Yolan.

"All I know is that man wants to buy a multi-million dollar property, so that's what I'm going to help him find," she said, glaring at each of them in turn. "Now, can we get to discussing these babies and baby showers or something else, please? Because the subject of Ryan Devoe is closed as far as I'm concerned," Yolan said drinking her water, refusing to acknowledge anything else they said about Ryan, especially how big he was.

"Fine, let's give her a few weeks, Asia. Then we will revisit the fact that she is dying to show him her very own million dollar property," Tayana said, throwing Yolan a wicked smile.

Yolan grabbed her water bottle off the table and stormed off towards her office.

"Both you horny, hormonal, huzzies can go straight to hell!" Yolan snapped, closing her door behind her.

Her phone vibrated on her desk, it was a text from Ryan: *'I enjoyed today, looking forward to working with you, Yolan'*

"Well fuck," Yolan mumbled to herself, tossing her phone back on the desk.

Chapter 3

"How many units in this one? I'm sorry, I left my copy of the listing at the office," Ryan asked and explained, a few days later, while looking over Yolan's shoulder at her iPad.

He was standing close behind her and his cologne traveled around her like a warm hug. They were standing in the lobby of the third hi-rise he wanted to see.

"This one will have 220 units, three pools, two gyms and a roof-top garden and lounge area when it's finished," Yolan replied looking over the listing and taking a few steps forward to put more space between them.

They had spent the last two days together and she was learning that Ryan was nothing like the stuck up, button-downed brother she'd thought he was. While he was 100% about business and acquiring his property, he actually was a pretty chill person with a great sense of humor.

He was an investment banker who traveled all over the world, his favorite being a tie between Dubai and Asia. He, like Yolan, was fluent in Mandarin, French, and Spanish but he also spoke Arabic and took the time to make sure she knew he had her beat by one language.

His funniest habit, she'd noticed so far, had to be him belting out random song lyrics when they popped in his head. He had a beautiful voice. After watching him walk around the lobby for a few minutes taking in the construction and crafts-manship of the building, she pushed the button to call the elevator.

"How many units are complete?" he asked leaning on the empty guard's desk.

His eyes lit up as he allowed them to take a leisurely stroll up and down her body while they waited for the elevator. His easy, slow, sexy smile spread across his handsome face when his admiring gaze met Yolan's hostile glare, he cleared his throat blushing at getting caught again and lowered his gaze to the floor.

"According to my last conversation with the seller 120 units are complete, as well as the roof-top garden and lounge area, both gyms and two of the three pools. You ready to go up?" Yolan stated and asked in an icy, but business-like tone.

Him, his wandering eyes, and stepping into her space was getting old or at least she was good at acting like it was. When, in reality, his eyes on her were like a tender caress that had her wanting more than she was ready to admit at the moment.

He followed her into the elevator, his smile still plastered in place. She could see his eyes were glued on her ass when she snuck a look at him over her shoulder.

"Excellent, let's start at the top and work our way down," Ryan suggested taking the copies of floor plans Yolan held out to him, she always had hard copies on hand. It kept him from having to get too close.

"Fine. Just so you know, there are some floors with no access because of construction and there are only four of the seven floor plans to see, the other three are in the incomplete units," Yolan explained, pulling out her stylus pen to jot down any questions or concerns he might have.

The elevator opened at the very top floor of the building, a foyer with a wall of glass doors stood in front of them. Beyond the doors were three ornate iron steps and an open space filled with top-of-the-line outdoor seating all made out of cherry wood frames and hunter green, all-weather cushions.

There were columns of flower-filled flower boxes of various sizes scattered all around and under a greenhouse-like covered area with an actual herb garden.

The shiny chrome lids of the custom-made BBQ grill, which was built into the entire length of the south wall, reflected the light from the sun, causing them to squint until their eyes adjusted. Ryan moved down one of the paths to look out at the view from the rooftop.

Yolan turned in the opposite direction and began to walk down the wooden walkway lined with wildflowers, she heard gurgling water and was curious to find the source. At the end of the path, there was another seating area, a circular one that surrounded a fire pit, the wall immediately behind it had a waterfall that ran down into a small pond with koi fish in it.

Yolan sat on the edge of the brick wall that surrounded the pond, taking in the smell of the flowers and the sound of the water flowing, while waiting for Ryan to finish looking around. As she waited, she thought over the other amenities and made note of what floor they were on to make sure they saw them all.

"Someone has an admirer," Ryan said, quietly walking up to her.

She immediately gave him a hard and impatient look until she noticed he was pointing at the pond. A curious koi fish was peeking out of the water looking up at her.

"Wow, how cute is that! I guess it must be the bright colors on my shirt that attracted him, or maybe it's close to feeding time," Yolan said, smiling, looking down at the koi, who still had its gaze trained on her.

"Or maybe he finds you attractive. You are a very beautiful woman, Yolan. It would be hard not to," Ryan stated, sitting down next to her on the edge of the pond. He reached up and softly pulled a small flower petal from her hair while looking into her eyes.

Immediately, the koi slipped back under the surface of the water and moved to the other side of Yolan and away from Ryan.

Yolan broke their eye contact and stood up, chuckling at the koi. Her heart rate sped up a bit and she started to sweat, in spite of the cool autumn breeze blowing around them and the cool mist rising from the waterfall and pond.

"Well, on that note, shall we move on and let him nurse his broken heart?" she suggested, straightening her skirt and moving quickly back up the path and to the elevator. What the hell was wrong with her? All he did was pull a flower petal from her hair and she was all hot and bothered. Yeah, she needed to help this man find his hi-rise before she lost what was left of her mind!

"This is it," Ryan declared, walking around the penthouse of the same property an hour later. His eyes were dancing excitedly as he rushed from room to room opening doors and closets.

Yolan looked up from her phone and blinked rapidly in confusion. She had been answering emails and ignoring teasing texts from Tayana and Asia, giving him space to see the penthouse.

"Ryan, we still have three showings tomorrow, perhaps you should wait until you've seen them all before making a decision?" she suggested, walking over closer to him.

As much as she needed this to be over with, especially with her reaction to him just touching her hair on the rooftop, her first priority was to her clients and making sure they ended up with exactly what they were looking for in a property with no compromise.

"We can cancel the other showings, this is the one. What's the asking price again?" he asked, strolling around the kitchen, nodding in approval of the marble countertops and stainless-steel appliances including the custom made Samsung Smart double oven.

Yolan looked from him to her iPad with a sigh, she really felt he should at least look at the other properties first. But it was his call.

"This one is the most expensive of the listings, the asking price is $650,000,000," she informed him quietly.

"$650,000,000? That's it? I would have thought $850. How soon can you get the paperwork started?" he asked, grinning like a kid on Christmas, still walking around checking everything out.

"I can get it started this afternoon. Do you have any questions or concerns I need to have addressed before we proceed?" Yolan asked, highlighting the seller's contact information and sending it to her email.

"Just one, when can I take you to dinner?" Ryan asked softly, moving closer to her. He took his eyeglasses from his face and tucked them into a case, then into his jacket pocket. He looked down at her, his honey brown eyes a bit darker than they were a moment ago.

"You can't. I never blur the lines between my professional and private life," Yolan answered, her stylus pen poised to write. She was fighting to keep her voice from betraying the fact that the way he was looking down at her had a shiver going up her spine.

His slow, sexy ass smile spread across his face as he nodded moving even closer. "I figured you'd say something like that, but hear me out. Once you close this deal for me our business will be complete, correct?" he asked softly, taking her hands in his. His tongue darted out and wet his bottom lip causing her stomach to dip. Fuck he was sexy!

"Technically, yes. But the fact will remain that we have a working relationship. My business did business with your business and might do more business one day. You never know what the future holds, so it would be foolish to cross that line," Yolan argued looking up at him and pulling her hands away.

"Hmm, good point but, nonetheless, we are both adults and know how to handle ourselves and set clear boundaries if necessary. So this makes your argument pretty baseless if you think about it. I don't like to beat around the bush, Yolan, so let me very clear. I want to get to know you better and, more importantly, I want you, period. I am very used to getting what I want, so think about what I said and after you close this deal for me, we will revisit this conversation. Be forewarned, I'm not one to take 'no' for answer when I really have my heart set on something," Ryan informed her, looking down at her seriously before opening the door to the penthouse and following her to the elevator.

Yolan rode down the elevator silently messing with her bottom lip, staring straight ahead, cussing herself out in her head. If she wasn't interested in him, like she kept telling Tayana and Asia, why wasn't she cutting his ass down like she normally did with unwanted attention? In the back of her mind, she heard the answer to her question and chose to ignore it.

"Yolan? You never answered me upstairs. Something else I have zero tolerance for is being ignored," Ryan said, stopping her in the lobby as they exited the elevator and she tried to make a hasty escape.

Yolan sighed deeply and looked up at him, his eyes connected with hers as she spoke. "Ryan, like I said, it's not a good–" Yolan started to argue her point again, when Ryan leaned down and pulled her into his arms, kissing her softly on the lips.

Her feet were barely touching the ground. Her knees went weak, as his soft lips came in contact with hers. Her ears were ringing so loudly it drowned out her voice of reason completely.

A low moan escaped from Ryan as he put her back solidly on her feet and moved backwards towards the door.

"Like I said upstairs, we will revisit dinner another time. In the meantime, I look forward to closing this deal, talk to you soon," Ryan stated with that sexy ass smile and a wink before leaving her standing in the lobby of the building speechless and trying to catch her breath.

Two weeks later

"Monet! Where you at, girl?" Yolan called, letting herself into Monet's place, a bottle of Dom in one hand, two slices of vanilla bean cheesecake from the Cheesecake Factory in the other one.

They were celebrating Monet and Shay's new clothing line deal and her and Royalty closing on one of their biggest deals ever, Ryan's deal.

She invited Asia to join them but she and Tayana were

going baby shopping, and Shay was having a private celebration with her man of six years, Butter. So tonight it was just her and Monet.

After a quick toast at the office she burned rubber to Monet's; she didn't even bother to stop by her house to change. Yolan argued with herself, the whole way, that her hasty retreat from the office had nothing to do with Ryan and his chill inducing lips.

She slipped off her shoes, dropping them by the door and rushed across the living room to the kitchen to put the cheesecake in the fridge and grab glasses, singing to herself.

Monet silently descended the carpeted stairs looking like she was going out, and not spending an evening at home. Her hair and makeup were flawless as always. "Hey, Yo, look at you! Looking like a fashionista in that Monet and Shay original," Monet commented, taking notice of Yolan's pale yellow pantsuit she wore to Ryan's closing.

He couldn't stop staring at her during the entire forty minute meeting, the trustee facilitating the sale had to bring his attention back to signing the paperwork several times. When they were done, she quickly shook his hand in congratulations and left as he was speaking to the seller.

"You know I gotta represent for the crew. Three people have complimented and asked me about this suit. So you and Shay need to get ready, those orders are about to start pouring in and not just from us," Yolan informed her popping the cork on the Dom.

"That's what I like to hear, but you do realize I made eggplant parmesan at your request, right?" Monet asked walking into the kitchen to check her pots before frowning over at Yolan.

"Yes, I'm aware of that, Monet. What's your point?" Yolan asked, after pouring champagne in both glasses.

"You are not going to eat in that suit, that's my point. You better carry your ass upstairs to the guest room and throw on some yoga pants, a sports bra or something. Why didn't your goofy behind go home to change before you came over here anyway?" Monet asked, fussing and cutting a loaf of French bread for their dinner.

Yolan blushed, thinking once again about Ryan and his kiss, and took a huge gulp of champagne.

Monet looked over at Yolan, her eyes narrowed as she caught on. "Girl! You mean to tell me you... you, Miss Yolan Belle, one of the baddest, coldest females I know is still running scared from a strait-laced investment banker! He's a Buppie, Yo, and he has you running scared? Wow," Monet said, shaking her head in amused amazement as she put the bowl of bread in the center of the table.

"You just don't underst— You know what? Fuck you, Mo! Your track shoes stay smoking from the way you are always running from Diamond, so who are you to talk?" Yolan snapped, storming across the living room to the stairs.

"That's different, Yolan and you know it. Diamond just invested 5.5 million in branding for me and Shay's clothing line so we are still in business, you and the Buppie? Did you or did you not close his deal today?" Monet argued, putting more dishes on the table.

"You know we did, Mo, that's part of the reason we are celebrating," Yolan answered, rolling her eyes, her back against the wall by the stairs with her arms folded, knowing what Monet was driving at.

"Then your business with him is done. So there is no longer a conflict of interest, now is there?" Monet reasoned, looking over at Yolan while leaning forward on the kitchen island sipping her glass of champagne.

"Oh shut up, Mo! You, Tay, and Asia, I swear y'all keep on working my damn nerves lately," Yolan snapped and stormed up the stairs to change, her eyes burned with frustrated tears she refused to let fall.

She wished she could tell Monet what the real problem was, all of them actually, but it didn't matter now because her business with Ryan Devoe was complete.

Chapter 4

"Good evening, ladies. Thank you for agreeing to meet later in the day, this morning sickness ain't no joke! Anyway, I know we have a lot to cover so let's get started. Besides, the smells Ms. Lanie has coming from the kitchen are killing me!" Tayana joked and smiled down the table at her ladies. Even though their operations had merged with Jazz's, they still held their weekly meetings with just the original crew.

"Where are we on the Freeze/Blue crew situation?" she asked, looking down the table at Joy and Rini.

"They left Houston but haven't set up anywhere else that we have seen, looks like they are underground," Joy reported, moving the print outs of the last correspondence with their lookouts down the table to Tayana.

"Hmm, they might be underground, but I honestly think they're plotting something. Look into that more closely, be thorough and check in every place they've been spotted and dig deep. From what I heard, Blue flipped on Freeze pretty quick so with his weak loyalty he's even more of a threat," Tayana ordered reading the papers Joy just gave her.

"Will do. Do you want us to stay with the lookouts we have or send some new faces?" Rini asked pulling up their roster at The Firm.

"All new, we got to keep them on their toes. Send some of Jazz's people too. I know our ladies are lethal but I want backup just in case. We also need to recheck any new movement here in case they were stupid enough to double back," Tayana said calmly, putting the paper to the side.

"Now then, I can report the expansion on the gallery will be completed in six weeks. The security room is state of the art with constant surveillance and quick access to anywhere in the gallery. Jazz wants constant security at all times rotating out every four hours. All the businesses are being upgraded to have one of our security teams on site at all times," Tayana informed them sitting back waiting for the barrage of questions to begin.

"Hold up, what's going on, Tay? I mean what happened, because we have never placed anything but flashlight cops at the businesses?" Yolan asked sitting up in alarm.

Tayana sighed and took a sip of her water that was next to her. "My brother, Man, happened. After all these years of wanting nothing to do with the business, he wants in. But after checking on his past – he has a bad track record – several failed businesses and owes money everywhere due to his drug use. I declined his offer to join us and well, he's been tossing our father's name around and now some of Heavy's old crew is backing him. He may present a problem," she told them looking at each one of the ladies.

"What are our orders if they show up or try approaching us on the street?" Jaidyn asked, assuming she knew the answer but, since it was Tayana's brother, she needed to be clear where they stood.

"Do what we do best, make them disappear. That order

includes my crooked, junkie ass brother, too," Tayana answered coldly without hesitation.

The crew nodded in agreement and pulled out their reports for the week.

"Yolan, you're up first, construction begins Tuesday morning," Tayana said and turned her chair to face Yolan, smiling as if the last five minutes never happened.

"I cannot believe you and Tay are now due on the same day, that is so crazy. I told Tay she was showing really fast, now both my god babies are due on the same day! I can't wait to start spoiling them!" Yolan said, clapping her hands excitedly while sitting in her office about a week later. Asia was sitting on the couch Yolan had custom made for her office, her puffy feet up on a pillow, typing notes on her laptop.

Yolan had suggested Asia work from home until the work was complete for the security upgrade, but she refused to. Instead she just spent most of her time in her office with the door closed, or in Yolan's office on her comfy couch. Their part-time receptionist, Star was manning the phones and greeting the walk-ins, since the workers had to partially close the office to install the new security station and surveillance equipment.

"God help us, you are going to be out of control, I can already tell. Everything this girl already has is from her Auntie Yo, I know Tay's nursery is full too. Seriously though, we are so blessed to have you and the rest of the crew in our corner. I mean with Butchie traveling for work all the time it puts me at ease to know you guys are here for me and the little princess," Asia stated, her eyes filling with sentimental tears as she ran her hand over her swollen belly.

Asia's husband Butchie oversaw the ground shipping for

Jazz's side of operations, he and Asia met in high school and had been together ever since. It was funny that the first one of them to get married, married someone in the business but was not in the business herself.

"Asia, we know you ain't *in* the crew but we got you, girl, for life or longer, but damn you and Tay stop crying! Y'all are killing me!" Yolan teased scrolling on her laptop to the next client file.

"Mr. Bernard Jackson is the older gentleman looking to sell their family home due to Mrs. Jackson's early onset Alzheimer's, and her admittance to a nursing home. Mr. Jackson doesn't really want to sell but he cannot afford both the mortgage and the facility rent."

Yolan's mind went back to the distinguished older gentleman who walked in shyly. With his hat in his hands and tears in his eyes when he spoke of the home that had been in his family for four generations, and also about his wife, who he had been dating since the 8th grade, and who was losing more of herself every day.

"Are you thinking what I'm thinking, Yo?" Asia asked teary-eyed again.

"That Royalty is about to buy another piece of property and Mr. Jackson and his family are going to get to keep their home completely debt free?" Yolan asked leaning back in her chair smiling, she loved that Asia's heart was just as big as hers was.

"Excuse me, Yolan, there is a Mr. Devoe here to see you," Star's voice announced over the intercom.

Yolan sat up straight and her palms immediately began to sweat. Shit! She thought ignoring him had made him finally give up.

"Uh, Star can you let him know I'm in a meeting, and have him schedule an appointment for next week, please, because of the construction," Yolan responded, pressing the intercom button on her phone.

"Never mind that, Star. He's a priority client. Have him have a seat and she will be with him shortly, if he doesn't mind the noise and dust," Asia called out and slipped her feet back into her ballet slippers.

"Knowing you, you have probably been in contact with the bank that holds Mr. Jackson's mortgage, so please forward me all the information and I will follow up today and make an offer to purchase. And you can stop shooting daggers at me because that shit doesn't work with me. Besides me and you haven't even had so much as an argument since high school, you never could stay mad at me anyway so I'm not worried about you being mad at me now," Asia informed Yolan with a smirk. Besides there's the fact I'm carrying one of your god children so save all of that venom for the boys in the hood and talk to the man, damn! It's one dinner, Yolan, you sit, you make small talk, you go home," Asia snapped at her before smiling over and winking. "Of course, whose home you go to afterwards is strictly up to you," she added and opened the door to leave Yolan's office.

His cologne immediately filled the room and her nose, followed by the noise of construction down the hall. Yolan watched Star walk over with a cup of coffee and stand directly in front of Ryan asking if she could get him anything else while he waited.

"Star, I'm sure Mr. Devoe will be fine with the coffee. I need some contracts typed up before you leave today. Please follow me to my office," Asia ordered as she moved back to her own office.

Star quickly grabbed her laptop and followed Asia inside of her office and shut the door behind her.

Yolan took about a dozen cleansing breaths before moving out from behind her desk to go face Ryan.

"Ryan, what a surprise, is there something else you need Royalty to do for you?" she asked, reaching out to shake Ryan's hand. He ran his finger lightly down the palm of her hand before he grabbed it to shake. Chill bumps immediately popped up on her arms, her eyes locked with his, the mischievous smile he was sporting took her breath away.

"Good to finally see you again, Yolan. There was one last loose end you forgot to tie up, could we discuss it further in the privacy of your office perhaps?" Ryan quipped, referring to her being MIA for almost a week.

When he licked his bottom lip before catching it between his teeth briefly, she knew he was remembering his stolen kiss.

"Of course, please excuse the mess. We are doing a bit of remodeling in the back but the dust seems to find its way everywhere, so we decided to reschedule all appointments until next week," she explained loudly over the noise of a table saw, glaring at him before turning on her heel and leading him through the small walkway to her office.

As per usual, she could feel his heated gaze glued to her ass. She motioned for him to sit in one of the plush purple chairs in front of her desk as she sat behind it.

"Now, how can I help you, Ryan? What loose end did I forget to tie up?" she asked. "As you can see and hear we are in no position to see clients this week but I will be more than happy to follow up with you next week," Yolan stated, smiling smugly over at him, knowing good and damn well what he was talking about.

"Are you avoiding me, Yolan? Did one little kiss send you running?" he asked, sitting back, looking serious and annoyed.

"No, actually I've been ignoring you, Ryan," she stated matter of factly, crossing her legs and folding her hands in her lap. "As I told you before, I do not mix my business life with my personal life, you just didn't listen. As far as that little kiss you referred to, it wasn't all that, and I have recovered from it just fine so don't flatter yourself," Yolan snapped, hoping to wipe the smile off of his face, but he only smiled wider.

"Hmm, if it wasn't all that, Yolan, why did you need time to recover from it?" he asked, rubbing his chin and looking over at her, smirking. "And if memory serves me correctly I told you, two things I don't like are the word 'no', especially when I am determined to have something or in this case, you, and being ignored. I'm not sure if you didn't take me seriously the first time, or now, but either way, if you pull a stunt like this again, I guarantee that beautiful ass of yours will be on fire.

"Let me tell you something else about me, Yolan. Normally, I'm just like you. Mixing business and pleasure is something I would never consider doing, never, that is, until I met you. From the moment you hinted I should take my business elsewhere, I have thought about you and wanted you. For the record I never went to another realty company, I simply did my research and asked around.

"No one has ever talked to me the way you did, and, until you, I would never do business with someone who did. And just so you know, that kiss? It stays on my mind. I have never asked a woman out more than once and I won't ask you again. I will simply come back and take what I have decided now belongs to me. Now, I suggest you take the easy way out and bend to my will as we both know way down deep that's what you want to do anyway," Ryan stated calmly with an air of confidence while looking over at Yolan who looked completely unbothered.

His eyes were shining behind his glasses, she could see the tip of his tongue peeking out the corner of his slightly parted lips. Yolan stared at his handsome face taking in all he just said to her. All she heard was no woman had ever stood up to him before so she presented a challenge nothing more, once the novelty wore off he would be on to the next one that tickled his fancy. And the way he kept trying to claim her... what the hell was that about?

On the other hand, she had to admit that something inside of her liked the idea of being claimed by Ryan Devoe and her mind drifted back to his statement about warming her ass up. The imagery alone had her juices flowing and her mind going to some places she never even knew existed inside of her and she was anxious to know more about them.

"Fine, Ryan, I will go on one date," she reluctantly agreed sitting back in her chair.

His sexy smile spread across his face, and his eyes lit up again. "When and where would you like to go?" he asked, leaning forward on her desk, taking her small hand into his.

"I need to check my schedule, I will let you know by this evening," Yolan stated, pulling her hand back and standing up to walk him back to the lobby. When he stood to his full height looking down at her with those damn eyes she felt a pull behind her belly button.

Once she stepped from behind her desk, before she could even think to react, he suddenly sat back down and pulled her to him, they were almost eye to eye because she was still standing. His mouth crashed down on hers, he grabbed the back of her head forcing his tongue all the way into her mouth.

When she put her hands on his chest and tried to half-heartedly push him away from her, he pulled her into his lap and wrapped his arms around her holding her in place. She felt his massive hands palming her ass and pulling her closer as he continued to feast on her mouth. This was nothing like their first kiss, this one was predatory and raw; he was reminding her of what he said a few minutes ago, he was claiming her as his.

She felt her nipples getting hard and pressing against the satin cups of her bra, her middle growing wet as he moved from her mouth to her neck and back again. Her ears were playing tricks on her, she swore she heard sopranos singing and her entire body tingled as he continued to kiss her like his life depended on it. His hands moved down to her bare legs, massaging her calves as he continued to kiss her.

Yolan grabbed the back of his head and forced her tongue into his mouth to taste him too, a low moan vibrated in his chest and rose up his throat as he tore his mouth from hers to catch his breath.

"Damn, my bad, Yolan. I just had to make up for that last kiss, you know the one that wasn't 'all that'," he growled still holding her in his lap, she felt him growing harder beneath her by the second.

She was panting, trying to catch her breath as she looked down at herself. Even with her bra on, her nipples were poking through her blouse and her chest was rising and falling as wave after wave of want rolled through her. She noticed her arms were wrapped around his neck, but more importantly, she took in the fact she was perched directly on his erection.

Yolan jumped up out of his lap quickly, blushing from the tips of her toes to the roots of her hair, folding her arms over her breasts. Her heart pounded against her ribcage, as desire rolled through her body, her middle throbbed and grew even wetter as she looked over at him, his honey brown eyes dark with want.

"Umm, like I said before, I will check my schedule and get back to you," she managed to say while rushing over on shaking legs and grabbing her suit jacket from the hook behind the door, pulling it on and buttoning it, to hide her nipples which were seeking him out like searchlights.

Ryan stood up slowly, looking down at her, his eyes dark and hungry, his erection pressing against his slacks begging to be freed.

"You do that, no disappearing this time. Better be sooner rather than later, ain't no telling what frame of mind I will be in if I have to come hunt you down again," He threatened gruffly and left her office, closing the door behind him.

"Okay, so I love this skirt on you with the white blouse with the puffy sleeves but is it sexy enough for a first date?" Tayana asked quietly, looking down at the fifteenth article she pulled from Yolan's walk-in closet three nights later.

Yolan sat on her bed silently shaking her head. Khrys and Jaidyn had done her hair and nails earlier that day on Tayana's orders, Asia drove her there to make sure she kept the appointment.

"Tay, this is a lot 'to do' about nothing. I am only going out with Ryan to get the novelty of me out of his system, once he sees we have nothing in common in any way, shape, or form he will take his balls and go home and leave me the hell alone," Yolan declared, admiring the blush color on her fingers and toes, at least when she told Ryan to kick rocks she would look flawless doing it.

"Yo, I am not even entertaining you and your particular brand of bullshit at this moment. The man likes you and you know it, and if the watered-down version of what you told me happened in your office the other day is true, then there is so much more than *like* going on so save it," Tayana snapped, tossing three more outfits on the bed.

"Whatever, Tay and, for the record, when I asked you to come over and pick me something to wear I didn't mean for you to empty my entire closet out onto my bed! Now will you pick something please? Damn!" Yolan fussed sitting back against her wall of pillows on her headboard.

Tayana pulled her burgundy wine colored hi-low, spaghetti strap dress that crisscrossed in the back out of the pile of clothes on her bed and tossed it at her.

"This one. Wear your burgundy suede pumps with the ankle straps and your medium sized gold hoops. You have a necklace from Rini that matches them and drops perfectly in your cleavage for the cut of that dress," Tayana ordered gathering up the clothes she had tossed on the bed to hang them back in the closet.

"Tay! This is a 'freak-him' dress if I ever saw one. I forgot I even had this, are you sure?" Yolan asked, holding the dress up, she would have to wear a thong or no panties with the way it caught the light.

"Yep, I'm sure. Put it on while I grab the jewelry so you can go, I am not letting you out of my sight until you leave for dinner," Tayana said, in her no nonsense way, walking over to Yolan's vanity and jewelry cabinet.

"What? Why, Tay? I am capable of dressing myself you know!" Yolan snapped, sounding outraged, coming out of her bathroom in the dress barefoot.

"Because I know your stubborn ass, that's why. I am going to make doubly sure you don't wait until I leave and change into a boring ass business suit or something," Tayana argued, handing Yolan the jewelry she wanted her to wear and the box that held her pumps. "Now go get dressed, or you'll almost be late."

"Damn, Tay, what the hell is up with you? It's a first date, not my freaking wedding!" Yolan took the shoes from her and slipped them on and walked over to the full-length mirror.

Twenty minutes later, her reflection took her own breath away, she looked stunning. Tayana's wardrobe choices were perfect! The burgundy dress went perfectly with her skin tone and with the hair and makeup style the ladies had done on her, she looked flawless.

"See, Yo? I told you. Now go get your man!" Tayana said loudly, pushing her out the door and into Ryan's arms or at least that's what she hoped.

Yolan couldn't fight the smile that instantly lit up her face as she pulled up to Vic and Anthony's steakhouse and saw Ryan standing out front waiting for her. He looked fine as hell in his black jeans and dark gray dress shirt.

His anxious smile spread into his full-fledged sexy one when he stopped pacing and saw her car pull up, he strolled over and opened her door before the valet could.

"God damn!" the valet swore under his breath after whistling through his teeth at Yolan, when Ryan helped her step out of her car.

"Watch that shit," Ryan hissed, shooting the valet a deadly look before handing him Yolan's car keys.

"You do look incredible, Yolan. I was kind of nervous you were going to stand me up. Seeing you in that dress, though? Definitely worth the wait," Ryan leaned down and whispered to her, his large hand was in the middle of her petite back as he escorted her inside the restaurant.

"So, you're an only child? No surprise there," Yolan quipped, taking a bite of her pasta. To her surprise, she and Ryan had much more in common than just overactive hormones.

The last hour had been filled with funny childhood stories and getting to know each other type questions. They had a very good conversation completely in Mandarin and he blew her mind again when he told her he was fluent in Japanese and Korean as well. He explained that in his line of work most of his clients were from Asia and it helped to speak their language, it made them feel more comfortable doing business with him because he went that extra mile.

"Why do you say that?" Ryan asked with a chuckle after chewing a bite of his New York strip steak.

"Your attitude has that only child vibe. 'I want things the way that I want them, when I want them, or I will go someplace else, me, me, me'," Yolan mocked with a deep voice, laughing when he threw her a maddening frown.

"Watch that shit, Yolan, you are coming dangerously close to me putting something on your ass," he warned and went back to chewing his steak. "Anyway, what is your middle name?" he asked out of the blue, he wanted to know all he could about her, just when one question popped in his head he followed it up with five more.

He liked this side of Yolan. Normally she was so controlled, almost cold, but tonight she was actually funny, actually warm, actually giving him a chance. Not that he had really given her a choice otherwise.

"Why do you want to know?" Yolan asked teasingly, taking about her fourth sip of her wine. Like the rest of the crew, she was careful to always stay in her right mind and never altered.

"Well, because everyone in your world calls you Yo. I want to call you something that only I call you and Lan ain't it. Honestly, I just don't think Yo fits this soft, gentle side of your personality you're showing me now," Ryan reasoned looking over at her, fighting the urge to let his gaze wander to her cleavage for about the millionth time.

"See? Only child energy right there! I have to have my very own special name for you," Yolan teased again with a mock deep voice, laughing a little.

Ryan leaned over and pulled Yolan's chair, with her in it, right next to him, his hand slid down her back to her ass where he rested his large hand, patting it lightly. "Keep it up if you want to," he told her in a no-nonsense way. "Now, I asked you a question, and why you gotta be so difficult all the damn time, Yo Lan?" he asked, over pronouncing her name and chuckling as his slow smile spread across his face. He was sure he had made his point so they could go back to having fun and getting to know each other better.

"Ugh fine. My full name is Nyiesha Marinna Yolan Belle," Yolan informed him, blushing a little at letting him know her full name. His threat had her second heartbeat thumping like crazy between her legs.

"A beautiful name for a devastatingly beautiful lady, it's interesting that you choose to go by the last of your middle names," Ryan said softly running his finger down the side of her face, down her neck to her shoulder and her arm. Chill bumps followed his finger's trail.

"You have some of the softest skin I have ever felt. My first fantasies of you were of me touching you all over, my fingers lightly skimming those beautiful legs of yours," Ryan admitted. His voice was whisper soft.

Yolan stared over at him smiling shyly at his compliment. A shadow fell over their table, breaking in on their moment.

"Aw shit is that my girl? I thought that was you! What's up, Yo?" Tayana's brother Melvin aka 'Man' exclaimed pulling a chair over to their table and flopping down in it, completely uninvited and ignoring Ryan.

Yolan immediately sat up straight on alert, her first thought was how to get Angel out of her purse and into her hand quickly and without Ryan noticing.

Her phone had been resting face down on the table and with one quick, almost invisible move, it was now unlocked and, in her lap, she pressed 3 on speed dial, the number to Joy and The Firm.

"Word on the street is you running things, is that true? Did Whisper really turn the reins over to you?" Man probed, his hard, blood-shot eyes boring into hers, the hostility he was tossing her way was barely contained. He was twitching, his nostrils flared as he sneered at her, she could see he had a gun tucked into his pants.

"Like that is any of your muthafucking business, Man. I can't believe you are dumb enough to approach me or even think you could try to pressure me to get to Jazz and Whisper," Yolan stated turning to face him, her gaze deadly.

Man reached over and grabbed her wine glass and drained it. "Fuck my bitch ass sister and that fool Jazz! She's acting all brand new on her own flesh and blood but giving her crew all the spoils of our father's hard work!" he spat, looking Yolan up and down like she was trash on the street.

She felt Ryan's entire demeanor change, as he sat silently watching their hostile exchange getting more and more upset by the second. She was sure he wanted to come to her aid but she didn't need that, she needed him to leave, knowing Man was packing and high she needed Ryan to get somewhere safe.

Yolan's trigger finger itched to put a fucking bullet in Man's head for the crimes he committed against Tayana in the past. But even more so now for disrespecting her and the crew now. Spoils from Heavy, her ass! Tayana and the ladies built their shit from the ground up with no love or help from Heavy or her fucking brothers!

In the beginning every dollar they made was a business or degree bought, most importantly they made it together, always loyal and willing to go to war for each other. To have him talk out of the side of his neck like he knew what they had been through pissed her all the way off! She knew she had to remain calm, this was not one of their spots so she needed to de-escalate the situation with minimal damage and fuck his shit all the way up later.

Scanning the room she saw a few of Heavy's old heads watching them, they had been out of the game so long, they had lost the ability to blend into their surroundings, six of them were scattered throughout the restaurant but close enough to get to her if they wanted to.

Fuck! She needed to sound the alarm, like now. "Ryan, can you excuse me for a moment and let me finish up with Melvin, please?" Yolan asked, never taking her hostile glare off of Man and his sweaty ass face. Them drugs had his dumb ass tripping, fucking bum ass idiot!

Ryan scoffed and the look he gave Yolan told her she was way outside of her mind if she thought he was about to leave her there with Melvin. "A better idea is we both leave and let Melvin finish up with his damn self," Ryan snapped, looking Melvin up and down throwing his own hostile glare his way.

"Ryan, please let me handle this. I'll meet you outside in ten minutes," Yolan pleaded, casting a small smile his way trying to appear calmer than she actually felt. She pressed the speaker on her phone, while Melvin was distracted looking at Ryan, as he scoffed at her again and sat back in his chair defiantly, at least now Joy could hear what was going on.

Her hand discreetly slipped Angel out of her purse and onto her lap, next to her phone, covering it with her napkin. Feeling Angel in her grip made her feel a little more relaxed but still on high alert, she wanted to take him out so bad she could taste it, lowlife piece of shit and she needed Ryan gone like now!

"Yeah, get the fuck outta here boy, grown folks is talking!" Man slurred at Ryan, puffing up like he was intimidating.

Ryan laughed, a haunting, scary humorless laugh as he looked over at Melvin. "Brother, another time and another place, I would have already knocked you on your ass, but I'm going to be cool because it looks like you and my lady have something to discuss. I'm going to let you slide just this once."

Ryan, the charming investment banker she was used to was gone, leaving this glaring, dangerous looking stranger in his place. "Yolan, you got about five minutes before I'm dragging your ass out of here," he told her, his light eyes now dark and angry.

Yolan blinked and nodded silently at Ryan before looking around the dining room again, so far no one from The Firm had arrived yet. She didn't need this shit, if it wasn't for Ryan, and Heavy's boys surrounding her, she would already have stuck Angel in Melvin's doughy middle and taken him to finish their 'talk' outside, but it was obvious Ryan wasn't leaving without her so she was stuck.

"Playa, I don't know who the fuck you are, but you better ask some—" Melvin started turning in his chair towards Ryan.

"Shut the fuck up you high ass, dick riding bitch! You want to know why your sister wants absolutely nothing to do with you? Shit like this, you loudmouth cunt. You're making a fucking scene! Now I advise you to get your loud, sloppy ass up and get the fuck outta my face and take the has been, past their prime, wanna be gangsters with you before I let my Angel sing," Yolan whispered fiercely, lifting the napkin so he could see the muzzle of her gun aimed at him. Out of the corner of her eye she saw Ryan look quickly from the gun to her in surprise.

At this point, she was so angry it felt like she had fire rolling through her veins, this idiot had no idea how close he was to death.

Melvin looked from her to her gun and sat back, a toothpick rolling around in his mouth as he smiled over at her, while grabbing a piece of pasta off her plate with his thumb and pointer finger and dropping it into his mouth, before licking his dirty ass fingers as he chewed loudly.

"So it's like that, Yo? Look whose little ass grew up and grew some nuts!" he said, still being loud as hell.

People around the restaurant began to watch them and whisper. She noticed her waiter and who she assumed was either the owner or the night manager throwing nervous glances their way, as one of them pulled out his cell phone. This was bad, all bad and on top of everything else she would have to explain it all to Ryan, damn it!

"Get up and leave while you still can. I know you're holding, and about five people here are dialing 911 as we speak." Yolan crossed her legs, Angel cocked and ready, waiting for his next move.

By the count in her head, she had 2.5 minutes left before Ryan made good on his threat and made her leave the restaurant. His anger was palpable as his eyes bounced back and forth between her and Melvin as it was, shit, shit, shit!

Fuck, she prayed The Firm was on the way, this was an entire ass mess.

To her relief Man finally stood up and glared down at her. "Looks like my bitch ass sister taught you well, you are almost as ruthless as her ass. Give her a message for me, tell her I'm coming for my throne," he spat and staggered back over to some of Heavy's old head crew.

Yolan let out a long breath and tossed three one-hundred-dollar bills on the table to cover their bill after putting Angel back in her purse discreetly.

"Let's go," Ryan ordered through gritted teeth, snatching the money off the table and pressing it back in her hand. He pulled out his money clip, pulled off some bills, dropped them on the table and started to move her towards the entrance of the restaurant, she barely had time to grab her wrap as he rushed her outside.

"What the fuck was that all about in there, Yolan?" he demanded as soon as they were back outside standing by the valet. He was looking at the door like he wanted to go back in after Melvin, hostility seeping from his pores.

Yolan spotted one of The Firm's cars and breathed an instant sigh of relief. She caught Rini's eye as she rushed by her to enter the restaurant, Yolan muttered the word, "Seven" as she passed by her to tell Rini how many men were inside and then directed her full attention back to Ryan. He was so busy being angry and looking around that he missed the split-second exchange.

"Nothing that concerns you, Ryan, but still something I need to handle immediately. I'm so sorry but can we raincheck?" Yolan asked looking up at him trying to appear calm, her phone was vibrating in her purse non-stop.

"Raincheck? Hell no we can't *raincheck*, but you can sure as hell tell me what the fuck is going on, Yolan. What do you need to handle? Who was that loud, high asshole and how does he know you? Why do you look like you are on the brink of losing your shit?" Ryan demanded looking down at her, his arms folded, nostrils flaring angrily.

"Like I said before, it's nothing that concerns you, Ryan but I need to handle it. Now, please, no more questions. I need to go, I will call you tomorrow," Yolan stated before signaling the valet for her car. She knew it was Tayana blowing up her phone and she was sure to be fit to be tied.

Ryan snatched her to him. "Doesn't concern me? If it involves you then it involves me," he told her making her look at him.

Yolan wanted to scream out loud, this shit was actually happening! "Ryan, please, I will explain everything tomorrow, but right now I have to go."

She didn't bother to wait for Ryan to answer as she moved out of his grip and rushed around to the driver's side, as the valet pulled up in her car, and peeled out of the parking lot.

"Yo, what the fuck happened?" Tayana demanded as soon as Yolan cleared the threshold of her and Jazz's house, about an hour later.

Joy and Bruise met her on a side street a couple of blocks from the restaurant and had her drive one of The Firm's cars to Tayana and Jazz's place, she did the regular dip and dive down a few wrong streets to make sure she wasn't being followed.

"Are you okay, Yolan?" Jazz asked rushing down the stairs, his eyes scanned Yolan looking for injuries as soon as he was close enough to her. He looked even more upset than Tayana did. Once he saw Yolan was okay, Jazz sat down next to Tayana taking both of her hands in his in an attempt to calm her down.

"I'm good, Jazz, just got some major damage control to handle tomorrow," Yolan answered, annoyed and sitting on the opposite couch across from them, massaging her temples. She wasn't worried about Melvin and all of his bullshit, all she kept seeing was the hostile look on Ryan's face when she left him standing outside the restaurant. No matter how attracted she was to him, she knew the best thing to do was to break things off with him sooner rather than later, just like her gut told her in the beginning, he wasn't equipped to handle this kind of drama and honestly, she didn't want him anywhere near any of this type of shit. She quickly shoved the sad feelings that came with that thought down deep and shifted her brain back into lethal mode, she wanted Melvin's head on a platter.

"Yo, are you going to tell us what in the entire fuck happened?" Tayana asked, her voice was about two octaves higher than normal as she glared at Yolan.

"The date. The date happened, Tay! I was at dinner with Ryan, and Man just approached me right there in front of Ryan and the entire fucking restaurant bitching about you dogging him out and only showing love to the crew. I counted six of the old heads with him too, including Sugar Bear," Yolan informed her, looking over at Tayana who had pulled her hands from Jazz's and now had them clenched tightly in her lap. Samuel Stubbs aka Sugar Bear was Tayana's godfather.

"That snake-ass bastard! He held my hand at my mom's funeral, my own godfather, he knows how everything went down and now he's running with Man's stupid junkie ass? Fuck Sugar Bear and Fuck Man! I want to kill them both myself for stepping to you, period! If those bitches would have done anything to you... oh my God, where is Mary Jane! We are handling shit tonight!" Tayana raged surging off the couch to go grab her gun and take care of business.

Jazz grabbed her by the back of her shirt and pulled her back down next to him. "The only thing you are going to do tonight is calm the fuck down, Boss Lady. Joy, Rini and The Firm are already handling it, trust our team, baby and besides, we have no idea where he's squatting and until we do there ain't shit we can do. Heads will roll over this shit, but just not tonight," Jazz stated giving Tayana a hard look, placing his hand on her belly, in an attempt to calm her down again.

Yolan's phone rang with The Firm's ringtone.

"Yo, you good?" Joy demanded, sounding pissed off. Yolan could tell she was driving by the background noise.

"Yeah, I'm cool, I'm with Jazz and Tay, I made sure no one followed me," Yolan stated ignoring Tayana who was giving her a hard, expectant look.

"They disappeared by the time we got inside the restaurant, but we got the plate number off of the car watching your house, we figured they would try some slick shit. Your car is parked in the private garage at the Skyline district apartment," Joy informed Yolan.

Yolan caught another voice in the car, sounded like they

were giving orders. "Is Rini with you?" Yolan asked holding up one finger at Tayana when she started mouthing questions at her. Finally, she just put Joy on speakerphone so Tayana could hear what she was saying too.

"No, that's Meika, she's talking to Pain to make sure things are all cool at the gallery and Royalty, there were cars parked there too. Whisper was right as usual. They tried to go after the businesses, but I don't think they know about the salon and boutique yet. Rini followed your man home to make sure they didn't go after him. I already called Asia and told her not to go into the office tomorrow and assigned undercover security to watch the salon and boutique until we get the stations permanently in place."

"Good and fast work, Joy. I need my ladies at my house at 7 a.m., we have a lot to discuss," Tayana ordered and actually relaxed a little after hearing Joy took care of business as usual.

"I'll let everybody know, Whisper. Yo, did he say anything we might be able to use to find him?" Joy asked, still upset that Man got away, ten seconds later she walked in the living room hanging up her phone.

"Nothing other than what he told me to tell, Tay," Yolan said, grabbing her phone and turning it off, before sitting back massaging her temples, trying to alleviate the anger causing her head to throb.

"What fucking message?" Tayana demanded, her voice low and deadly, shooting daggers at Yolan, like she was Melvin and not her best friend and second in command for most of her life.

"He said to tell you he's coming for his throne," Yolan said, her eyes locking with Tayana's. They relayed an unspoken message to each other, both remembering the same day from the past instantly.

"*His* throne? All Heavy left was a bunch of bullshit and debt. Yeah, let him come for me, let him try to take what me and mine have built, I'll be waiting right behind that mutha-fucka to put a bullet in his fucking head! Junkie piece of shit!" Tayana hissed before storming out of the room and up the stairs that led to her and Jazz's bedroom.

"Joy, Yolan, I need you two to handle this, you and I know she is in no condition to get involved in this, even if she can't see it right now. I want all of them to be a memory as soon as humanly possible," Jazz instructed them after watching Tayana stomp up the stairs and slam their bedroom door.

"We got it handled, Jazz. As soon as we find the rat's nest they're holed up in, they will be," Joy promised handing Yolan the key to the apartment she would be staying in for the time being before walking out the front door.

"Are you sure you're okay, Yo? You know you're more than welcome to stay here tonight if need be. I know that shit is fucking with you," Jazz offered, moving off the couch to go upstairs with his pregnant wife.

"I'm fine, Jazz, just take care of our Boss Lady. Me and the crew got this handled. Anything else?" Yolan asked, looking over at Jazz, while getting ready to leave.

"Just be careful out there, Yolan. Desperate men are reck-less but drug fiends, like Man and Heavy's old crew, don't have shit to lose," Jazz warned walking her to the door.

"Shit, yeah they do, they still have their pulses. Me and the ladies gonna damn sure take care of that problem for them as soon as possible," Yolan promised as she left.

Chapter 5

"Yolan, this is Ryan, *again*, I have called you at least a dozen times in the last four days, and you know how I feel about being ignored but honestly, I just need to know you're all right. I tried going by your office, but it's locked up tight. I'm worried about you. Look, you don't even have to explain what happened the other night if you don't want to, just call me back, please."

Yolan sighed and re-saved Ryan's last message, tossing her phone back on her desk. He left that message over a week ago, she didn't return his call that day or any of his calls after that one either, he was a distraction she couldn't have in her life right now, or ever.

She knew he would never stop asking questions about the scene with Melvin at the restaurant which would lead to questions about her carrying a gun, questions about Tayana and the crew, questions about her absences when she had to be away handling business for the ladies and when she finally did answer those questions, she knew he wouldn't understand the answers she gave and why things in her life had to be the way they were.

Ryan didn't grow up in the world she did, her entire life she'd been surrounded by people like her, Tayana, Jazz and the crew. Her father laundered money for all the big money crews back in the day including Tayana's father, Heavy. Her mother ran drugs in and out of the country for years but was retired now, and her brother, Tone was a lookout for one of the local gangs in their neighborhood and was killed when he was sixteen.

While her family was not poor by any means, when her brother was killed everything fun like their family vacations, dining at fine restaurants, and amazing holidays came to a stop and honestly, with all of that, she never experienced the carefree childhood Ryan described on their date.

They were from two vastly different worlds so as much as it hurt to do it she would rather steer clear of him before she messed around and did something really stupid like fall in love with him and get her heart broken... again.

***

"I need them both delivered by Saturday, October 9th as we previously discussed, will they both be ready in time?" Yolan asked, regarding the custom-made bassinets she ordered for Tayana and Asia two months ago. She came in to make sure they were exactly what she ordered, both made of imported Italian lace, one in ivory and one in white.

"Yes, Miss Belle, they will be delivered by 10 a.m. on the 9th of October, will that work for you?" the owner's daughter confirmed, taking the card with the delivery address on it Yolan held out to her.

"Perfect. Please be sure to thank your father again for his beautiful work, my god babies deserve nothing but the best. I'm so happy he made the time to make these for them,"

Yolan said, smiling excitedly and turned to leave, and walked right into the person behind her.

"I am so sorry, I wasn't paying atten–" Yolan began to apologize and explain but stopped short, as she found herself staring into the honey brown eyes of Ryan Devoe.

"Well. Hell," Yolan mumbled looking up at him. Her dreams and fantasies of him had nothing on the live version, he was even finer than she remembered.

"Looky, Looky here, what a small world. Imagine running into the elusive Nyiesha Marinna Yolan Belle while shopping for an old-fashioned style rocking chair for my great aunt for her birthday," Ryan stated a lot calmer than he looked, he honestly looked like he was ready to kill her.

Yolan stared up at him silently while adjusting her stance and felt Angel pressing against the small of her back, an instant reminder of why she phased him out of her life.

Her greedy eyes scanned the face that had a permanent starring role in her dreams, even with his jaw set and eyes cold, he still knocked her off balance. In the couple of weeks since she last saw him, she noticed he had a few gray hairs now mixed in the dark brown hair of his beard; that change was sexy to her too.

"Hmm, still giving me the silent treatment I see. Maybe one day you will do me the courtesy of telling me what the hell that's all about?" he snapped quietly, looking down at her. His eyes were silently asking her a thousand or more questions as he continued to glare at her.

In his eyes she could see the moment when his anger shifted to want, as he drank her in from the top of her head to her ballet slipper wrapped feet. A split second later, he took her by her hand dragging her out of the furniture store.

Yolan snapped out of her trance and stopped walking, pulling her hand away.

"What the hell? Where the fuck do you think you're taking me?" Yolan demanded planting her fists on her hips.

"My first reaction is to wear your ass out with the palm of my hand before making you stand in the corner as punishment for making me worry like you did. But right now, more than that, I want to– no, I need answers, Yolan and I am determined to get them. Now, there's a coffee shop around the corner, so we can either go there and talk or continue snapping at each other in the furniture store, either way we are having a conversation," Ryan explained looking down at her, his face was void of any emotion.

"Well, you could have asked me, Ryan, instead of dragging me out of there like you were my damn daddy or something!" Yolan snapped glaring up at him. Why didn't he just take the hint and leave her the fuck alone? Not only was it what she wanted, it was what she needed. Being this close to him was killing her. Couldn't he see they had no business even trying to be together?

"No, not like your daddy, like your man, because that's what I am, Yolan, your man. Now we are going to have a talk, for as long as it takes to clear the air between us and get back on the same page, got it?" Ryan said, looking like he was barely holding on to his sanity.

Yolan calmed down a little and actually felt bad for snapping at him, it wasn't his fault that he grew up the way he had and could never understand her lifestyle, that familiar tug she felt when she was around him began to unfurl in her lower region.

"Got it. Lead the way," she finally said quietly. She saw her driver, Troop pulling up and waved him on, since the morning meeting after the 'Melvin' incident, Tayana had insisted on a security car and driver for Yolan. It was so hard to have to inform someone of every place she was going, meeting or planning to be.

She really missed the freedom of driving her own car, but to give Tayana peace of mind until this Melvin and Heavy shit was handled, she would just have to deal with it.

Ryan watched the town car turn the corner and looked over at Yolan with his eyebrow raised. "Friend of yours?" he asked gesturing in the direction the car went.

Yolan felt her face get hot, she needed this 'talk' over with a quickness, she hated having to answer to any fucking body! "Yeah, something like that, now where is this coffee shop?" Yolan asked, shrugging up at Ryan, looking defiant and hostile.

"Yeah, we will have to talk about that, too, and just follow your nose," Ryan said taking in a deep breath and pointing Yolan in the direction the rich scent of coffee was coming from.

"Wow, do you know how many times I walked right past this place? I never knew it was here," Yolan said as they sat down at a table in the back of the hole in a wall coffee shop.

"Yeah, that's one of the reasons why I love this place so much, not too many people know about it and they make a mean cup of coffee. I think the only coffee better than this is your office," Ryan said, taking a drink from his cup, smiling a genuine smile for the first time since they ran into each other.

"Good to know we are at least in the top five," Yolan quipped sipping her green tea, returning his smile and feeling calmer by the second just being with him again, the last couple of months had been hell.

Ryan stared at her still smiling, he reached over and took her hand. "Yolan, you're always number one, my number one, don't you know that?" he said softly, running his thumb softly across the top of her hand. "You and your happiness as well as your safety will always be important to me."

A shocking chill ran through her body at his gentle touch, she crossed her legs to combat the humming that had started between them. His words were like a gentle caress and every-thing she needed to hear, having someone care about and protect her was all she ever wanted but still alarm bells began low and grew until they began clanging loudly in her head. With the way her life was set up, they were not to be.

"Ryan, you said we came here to talk, in your exact words to 'clear the air', remember?" Yolan reminded him, pulling her hand away and folding them in her lap even as her body screamed out the need for contact, any contact with him.

"My bad. I forgot I'm dealing with the Ice Princess," he sneered sitting back in his chair. "I hope you know that funky little attitude does nothing but get you one step closer to getting that discipline I know you need. Fight it all you want, Yolan, you and I will be together," he told her with that emotionless gaze again. She immediately missed his teasing sexy smile.

"Whatever, Ryan, I don't have all day to exchange insults with you. You asked me here to talk, so talk," Yolan snapped, rolling her eyes in his direction.

"You got one more chance, Yolan and I'm snatching you out of that chair and wearing your ass out with my hand. Now just tell me what's up, tell me what's going on. You froze me out and I have no fucking idea why. I mean damn, Yolan was my breath kicking that night? Did I have a huge ass booger hanging? Food in my teeth? What the hell did I do that not talking to me period is the solution?" he asked leaning forward, putting his elbows on the table looking over at her.

Yolan blinked in disbelief, his first question wasn't about Melvin or any of that bullshit with her gun? All he cared about is why she stopped talking to him? No, this had to be a trick, he was going to try to get her to relax and then start cross examining her, picking her life apart.

"Hello? Anybody home? Yolan you in there?" he asked, waving his hand in front of her face and snapping his fingers.

"You know I hate to be ignored, if you don't stop testing my patience–" he warned taking another sip of his coffee.

"Oh damn, yeah I'm here, you just caught me off guard that's all. I was all but sure the first thing you would demand to know about is that scene with Man," Yolan admitted nervously rubbing her hands together under the table.

Ryan blinked a few times with a frown on his face, running that night through his memory bank. "Yeah, I was salty about that scene for all of about ten minutes, I was more focused on you and me and the dialogue we needed to have. So why would I keep pressing you about it? Whatever, that is your business until you want to make it my business, honestly I had pushed that whole incident out of my mind until you brought it up," Ryan said with a shrug finishing the last of his coffee.

Yolan pushed her cup of green tea to the middle of the table, she heard what he said but her mind wouldn't let her believe it. In her insecure fantasy world, he was judging her daily, thanking God he dodged the bullet of falling for a hood rat but in reality all he cared about was her not calling him back and what he did to cause it? Get the fuck outta here!

Ryan was watching her, patiently waiting for her to answer when the realization hit him. "Hold up! You mean to tell me the reason you've been treating me like dog shit on your red bottoms is because of what happened in the restaurant with that loud, drunk idiot?" Ryan demanded loudly sitting back up in his chair. They were the only ones in the coffee shop and the teenagers behind the register were too busy flirting with each other to notice Ryan beginning to get loud.

"Shh, keep your voice down and yes, that is part of the reason I stopped talking to you," Yolan admitted feeling her whole face getting hot with embarrassment.

"Wow, that's… that's um… that is stupid as hell, Yolan! I'm not stupid or conceited enough to think that you didn't have a life before you met me, I have a history too. Hell, mine might be even worse than yours," he told her looking like he was really about to snatch her out of her chair and make good on his initial threat to spank her, and the way her hormones were raging at the moment, she halfway thought she would welcome it. Him still claiming her as his was making her giddy and horny as hell at the same time.

"It's not like that. Man is a part of my past but not in the way you're thinking and—"

Yolan stopped herself and stood up to leave. This was not how any of this type of shit worked and no matter what her hormones and wayward thoughts were telling her, her common sense told her she was saving herself from the pain of heartache that was bound to come from dealing with a man like Ryan.

"And what, Yolan? I told you we were going to clear the air, and that is what we are going to do," Ryan said reaching over and taking her hand again, holding her in place as she stood next to the table with her back to him. "And a fun fact, you're not disappearing on me again, so get that thought the hell out of your head right now."

Yolan took a deep breath and looked over her shoulder at him and sighed. "And I-I didn't want you to judge me," she blurted out and dropped her head looking at her shoes. She felt his large hand loosen and drop hers.

"Damn, you didn't want me to judge you. Ain't that the exact damn thing you're doing to me?" Ryan demanded, his eyes dark and narrow. Yolan turned to face him, questions in her eyes.

"Huh? Of course not! I have never, would never judge you, Ryan, you just don't understand, and you never will," Yolan reasoned, shaking her head in the negative, frustrated with them both, they needed to pull the band-aid off of this wound already and call it quits.

Ryan stood up, looking down at her, his hungry gaze

taking in her form-fitting dress before raking over her bare legs and meeting her eyes again. "What don't I understand, Yolan? And how do you know I won't understand it? I'll tell you why, because you prejudged me without knowing how I will react to anything, without knowing me," he stated, shaking his head as he looked down at her. "I know you got some shit going on in your life, but like I said before until you make it my business, I don't give a fuck about any of it besides you and your safety and as long as you're safe and coming home to me, I have nothing to say about it," he told her with a shrug.

Yolan covered her face with her hands and let out a frustrated groan. "Ryan, it's just not that simple and no matter what you say, you don't get it. We will never work just please understand that, understand that and move on, I am not the girl for you."

Ryan stood up and looked down at her, his sexy smile shining through in spite of his frustration. "You're right, you're not the girl for me but you *are* the woman for me and it's beyond time you got used to that fact," he said reaching over and pulling her into his arms, his lips crashing down on hers.

His tongue wasted no time forcing its way inside her mouth and began to dance with hers, he pulled her tighter against him as their kiss deepened. He held her head in his hands and kissed her entire face, eyes, nose, cheeks, then her lips again, nipping her bottom lip lightly before pushing his tongue in her mouth and tasting her mouth again.

His hands slowly traveled down her body and jerked to a stop when his hand made contact with her gun. He pulled his lips away from hers looking down at her in question.

She forced her way out of his arms and moved quickly towards the exit.

"That look right there is exactly what I'm talking about. I

need to go, goodbye Ryan, for good this time," Yolan said over her shoulder, trying to catch her breath as she went.

———

Ryan sat down in annoyance as he watched Yolan, the woman he decided was destined to be his from day one, walk away from him again. He fought the urge to go after her, throw her over his shoulder, take her to his house and show her what they were going to be to each other, because he knew brute force was not the way to get what he wanted from her, and while he did want her to submit to his will, there was more than one way to make that happen. He knew one damn thing though; this would be the last time he let her walk away from him and not have any idea where she was going.

———

Yolan walked in the apartment and tossed her keys on the table and carried her takeout to the kitchen to plate it up. Just as she pulled out silver metal chopsticks and began to pour lomein on her plate, the doorbell rang.

Yolan dropped the food on her plate and laid the chopsticks next to it before quickly checking the doorbell camera on her phone. Ryan was standing in the hallway in front of her door.

"What in the actual fuck!" Yolan swore to herself as she snatched the door open glaring up at him.

Ryan quickly moved inside the apartment and took Yolan into his arms, lifting her off her feet, and before she could utter a word driving his tongue into her mouth. He walked further into the apartment moving to the living room with her in his arms.

She kicked air as she fought to get down, but he had her so tight in his grip, all she could do was be kissed.

He deposited her on the couch still kissing her, his hands ran down her back, and he quickly relieved her of Angel, setting her gun on the end table.

His mouth moved from her lips to her ear. "For the last fucking time, Yolan, I don't give a damn what's up with you until you tell me to. Now I know you carry a gun, and as long as you aren't aiming it at me we're cool, to be honest its sexy as hell," he growled in her ear before running his tongue around the edge of it.

His warm, soft lips dropped kisses down her neck causing her to moan despite the fact she was still trying to figure out how he found the apartment *and* got past security.

He laid her back and gripped her ankle, wasting no time lightly running his fingers up her soft legs. He kissed her softly on her ankle bone, then her calf, behind her knee and inner thigh.

She jumped at the contact of his soft lips on her skin, he lifted his head smiling down at her. "Should I continue, Yo?" he whispered teasingly, kissing her thigh again.

Yolan closed her eyes and threw her head back moaning, her pussy growing wetter by the second. "Yo? Since when do you call me, Yo?" Yolan asked, grabbing ahold of the couch cushions as his kisses moved higher and closer to her middle.

His finger hooked around the elastic of her lace panties, and he slid them down her legs...

"Yo! Girl, will you wake up? Damn!" Tayana snapped, pushing her head off of her pillow.

Yolan woke up with a start in the middle of her bed and sat up blinking over at Tayana confused.

"What the hell, Tay?" Yolan asked, looking around for the source of her dream, suddenly disappointed when she realized he wasn't really there.

"Shit, you tell me! I came by to make sure everything was okay because you didn't answer your phone and I get here and you're moaning and groaning, whispering Ryan's damn name!" Tayana sat down on the bed next to her smiling like the Cheshire cat.

Yolan lay back on the bed and covered her face with one of her pillows, blushing. It was a fucking dream? She could still feel every place his lips touched on her body. Her nipples were hard and her pussy was throbbing.

"So, tell me, Yo was he good?" Tayana teased, pulling the pillow from her face.

"Shit, I don't know, we hadn't gotten that far yet, thanks to your dream killing ass!" Yolan snapped playfully, hitting Tayana in the face with a throw pillow before climbing off of the bed and going to the bathroom.

"Damn, he hadn't even howdy ma'am'd the debutante and you were moaning like that!" Tayana called out after her.

"It's too early for this shit, Tay and why are you here anyway?" Yolan demanded washing her face with a cool fluffy washcloth standing in the bathroom doorway.

"Like I said you didn't answer your phone and I got worried, so I came over to check on you. Besides, Troop told Bruise about you meeting up with a tall man he'd never seen you with before, and you appeared upset after your conversation with him when he gave his report this morning," Tayana informed her, grabbing Yolan's phone, it was on silent, but she saw when it lit up with an incoming call.

"No wonder you didn't answer. Why the hell is your phone on silent?" Tayana demanded answering Yolan's phone.

Out of the entire crew, Yolan never silenced her phone, not even during down time or vacations just in case anything went down she would be ready.

"Because Ryan—" Yolan started to explain when Tayana

held up her finger as she listened to the caller on the other end of Yolan's phone, looking serious.

Yolan was quickly on alert, she rushed over to her closet and pulled on a pair of jeans and a random shirt.

She checked Angel and after making sure the safety was on tucked her in the small of her back under her shirt. She grabbed a pair of knee high boots and slid them on too.

"Where do I need to be?" Yolan mouthed to Tayana who was still listening to whoever was on the other end of the phone.

"Ryan, I'm sorry this isn't Yolan, it's Tayana. Yolan's best friend, hell I guess you can call me her sister. I would have told you before you let all of that out but you wouldn't let me get a word in. Anyway, is all that true? Is that how you really feel about her?" Tayana asked, smiling and quickly moving out of the way of Yolan's grabbing hands.

When she realized who Tayana was on the phone with, she tried to grab the phone from her, for a pregnant woman she was still pretty fast.

"Give me the phone, Tay!" Yolan hissed, glaring at her angrily.

Tayana sidestepped her and casually walked into the bathroom still chatting away, answering Ryan's basic questions and closed and locked the door behind her.

"Are you fucking kidding me, Tay?" Yolan screamed at the door before storming out of the bedroom.

She knew Tayana well enough to know once she decided to do something there was no stopping her, and she couldn't care less how angry Yolan got in the process. From the second she answered Yolan's phone, Tayana had decided to poke her nose in her business where Ryan was concerned, damn it! She had no idea how far Tay was willing to go with it and that made her nervous as hell.

"All right, Yo, spill it," Tayana demanded, coming into the

kitchen about twenty minutes later where Yolan was sipping chamomile tea to calm her frazzled nerves.

"What did he say to you?" Yolan asked quietly, walking over grabbing a muffin off a serving tray on the counter. She assumed Tayana had brought them with her, baked goods of any kind were her craving.

"Not important, now answer me, what's up, Yo? What is the real reason you keep pushing him away?" Tayana asked taking a muffin for herself before sitting across from Yolan.

"Almond milk or whole?" Yolan offered sliding off her island stool, grabbing a glass, ignoring Tayana's question.

"Whole and don't play with me, Yo. I know you, and you really like him, so why won't you stop playing with his emotions and just get with him?" Tayana asked, peeling the wrapper off of her cinnamon muffin and pinching off a tiny piece before setting the rest on the plate, Yolan just put in front of her along with a tall glass of milk.

"Tay, just leave it alone, it doesn't matter. Besides with all this shit with Man and the old heads I need to operate with no distractions," Yolan reasoned, playing with the wrapper on her own muffin.

Tayana's eyes narrowed as she slowly chewed her muffin and took a sip of her milk, taking her time as she processed Yolan's words. Yolan hated that look, she was in for some undiluted Tayana wisdom.

"It don't matter but here you sit, avoiding his phone calls while you call out his name in your sleep. The first words out of your mouth when I talked to him were 'what did he say to you?', how do you know I allowed him to say anything else, Yo? How do you know that I, being your sister friend, didn't shoot him down permanently for you?" Tayana asked finishing up her food, looking pointedly at Yolan.

Yolan's stomach dropped in fear. If Tayana told him to beat it, he was never contacting her again, period. The thought of never seeing Ryan again made her feel physically ill.

"Is that what you did, Tay?" Yolan asked. Her heart rate doubled as she tried to look nonchalant but, in all honesty, she was afraid to know the truth. She still had yet to touch the muffin resting on her plate.

"If it doesn't matter, why do you care, Yo?" Tayana asked, a small knowing smile on her face.

Yolan finished her tea and rinsed out her cup, after putting it in the dishwasher she walked into the living room flopping down on the couch.

"Whatever, Tay," Yolan snapped and sat back hard, her back to Tayana.

"You know I got all day, right? So, we can either get into this now and move on, or you can keep throwing daggers at me and we do this round and round shit until Jazz comes looking for me after the sun goes down," Tayana stated joining her on the couch.

Yolan shook her head annoyed, folding her arms. She loved and adored her best sister/friend but in this moment, she was getting on her damn nerves, she needed to leave it alone!

They sat, not speaking for the next hour, Yolan stubbornly silent, flipping channels, while Tayana sat humming a sweet tune, rubbing her hand on her swollen belly, waiting on Yolan to answer her, when the doorbell rang.

Yolan jumped up and pulled Angel from her back, looking over at Tayana in alarm.

"Relax, Yo, it's Monet. I texted her and told her to come by, I saw you are determined to be a stubborn ass and called for reinforcements." Tayana sat back and went back to humming to the baby.

Yolan sighed in frustration and rushed across the room

and let Monet in, she was dressed to the nines and fit to be tied.

"What's up, Yo? Are you really still doing this?" Monet demanded, storming in with two reusable grocery bags full of food and snacks.

Shit! Tayana wasn't playing, she was determined to get her to come clean about Ryan, there was enough food for the three of them to hunker down all night.

"Don't you start, Mo! I already have Tay in here all up in my business, humming happy tunes like Snow White and shit, I don't need you and your diva like attitude up in here too," Yolan grumbled as she helped her put food away.

"Damn, Whisper you were right, she got it bad!" Monet said, shaking her head over at Yolan, pouring herself a glass of sparkling water.

"Ugh! Don't both of you have something better to do but annoy the hell out of me? I'm saying don't both of you have businesses to run?" Yolan snapped, flopping back down on the couch and picking up the remote control to the TV. Monet sat down on the other side of her and placed her glass on a coaster, snatching the remote from her hand.

"Exactly! So stop acting like a damn drama queen and tell us what the fuck is up with you! Why are you pushing this man away when it's obvious you like him!" Monet snapped, turning off the TV and keeping the remote out of Yolan's reach.

"Why do you two even care? We have shit going on that is much bigger than my personal life. I have told you both before, Ryan Devoe is a distraction that I cannot afford in my life right now. Period. End of story." Yolan felt her face getting hot, her eyes beginning to sting, she kept reminding herself they were doing this out of love, but they still made her sick!

"So you say, but who are you trying to convince, Yo? Us or yourself? We are your family, girl, have loved you for life or longer and we know you are feeling this dude but, for some reason, you won't let your guard down to be with him, why is that?" Monet asked turning to face Yolan, folding her legs underneath her once she slipped off her shoes.

Yolan stared at the now dark TV and bit the inside of her cheek, she was not in the mood for this shit.

"Why can't y'all just trust my judgement like you always do and let this drop? Please. Tay, Mo, I just want to put it behind me," she said quietly looking down at her hands, fighting back the tears that wanted to fall.

"Yo, we do trust your judgement, we trust you with our lives you know that, but we know you and this is not about Ryan being a threat or a distraction. This is about something else, something you're not telling us, so what's up, Yolan?" Tayana asked her gently, taking Yolan's hands in her own.

"Tay, it's stupid and it doesn't matter, okay? Just trust me, this is for the best," Yolan pleaded as the first tears began to fall, taking her back to one of the worst days of her life, eight years ago.

"Deon please, I can explain," Yolan pleaded with her fiancé of one year, as he looked at her like he had no idea who she was.

For two years she had managed to keep both of her worlds separate from each other. To Tayana she was Yo, her second in command, willing to do what it took for their crew to continue to rise to the top.

To Deon she was Yolan, he hated the use of nicknames, found them childish and tacky, he also found her first name Nyiesha too ghetto to ever use, she was ambitious, up and coming, still taking night classes to earn her degree in communications while working as a real estate agent during the day.

In Deon's eyes she was the perfect woman to have on his arm, she dressed elegantly, spoke several languages, didn't challenge or question him on most things, and best of all, she was not what he considered a stereo-

typical black woman, she knew her place and was never loud and confrontational, never that is until that night.

"What can you possibly say to explain this, Yolan? You pulled a gun, an actual gun on my boss! I could hear you screaming insults at him from outside by the pool! Do you have any idea what kind of damage control I am going to have to do? I could lose everything I have worked for behind your ghetto acting ass!" Deon snapped with a disgusted sneer directed in her direction.

"Deon, he cornered me when I came out of the bathroom and put his hand up my dress and grabbed my crotch, ripping my underwear! He tried to fuck me in the damn hallway with you and his wife and everyone else down by the pool sipping drinks! I did what I had to do to protect myself!" Yolan explained pleading with him, looking at him feeling herself getting upset again by his reaction.

"Then you should have let him, took one for the team and we would have hashed the shit out another time. You knew how important this party was to my career," Deon said quietly sitting on the bed taking off his shoes. Yolan blinked in shock and disbelief did he actually just say that to her?

"I'm sorry, what? Did you just actually say I should have let your flabby, fat, swine of a boss rape me so you could get further in your career?" Yolan asked trying to remain calm, he had been drinking, maybe he didn't realize what he just said, she reasoned with herself.

"You heard me the first time, Yolan. I see no reason to repeat myself. Hell, I know all about your ghetto and hood rat past, you should have been humble and stayed in your place and thanked God that someone like me even gave you a second glance let alone a ring. You are just supposed to play the fucking game, but oh no, not you. The minute I let my guard down, you show your true fucking colors and tank my fucking career," he growled over at her removing his clothes and changing into his pajamas.

"All you had to do was be pretty, speak when spoken to in whatever language was spoken to you and not embarrass me, now I have to start all over because I picked the one fucking hood rat who thinks she's actually worth more! To make matters worse, sadly enough, I almost loved you

too!" Deon stated matter of factly, shaking his head looking at her in disgust.

"Almost," Yolan repeated quietly, seeing Deon for the shallow, self-centered person he actually was. The only thing that was keeping him alive was the fact that her gun was downstairs in her purse by the front door.

"Yeah, almost. You didn't actually think I was dumb enough to really love someone like you, did you? The only reason me or any man like me, for that matter, would give you a second glance is because you got a banging body and can string sentences together in several different languages, you were easy to manipulate and control until tonight, now you're just worthless, a waste of my fucking time!" Deon spat, feeling himself, stepping in front of her until he was in her personal space.

Yolan's eyes narrowed angrily as she kicked him in his knee, tearing the ligament that held his kneecap in place, it was now dislocated to the left side of his leg looking like a huge tumor. He dropped immediately looking at her in shock as he began to scream in pain.

"You crazy bitch!" he shouted, clutching his knee.

She threw two quick punches in rapid succession, one to his trachea, and another knocking out his two front teeth.

"A couple of things to know about women like me. One, we only need one time to learn to stay the fuck away from men like you and two, disrespect is never tolerated. Now shut the fuck up you weak pussy before the neighbors call the police," Yolan hissed as she stepped over him as he lay there in a slobbering, drooling bloody mess.

"Oh my God, Yo! How could you never tell me, tell us, about all of this? Where is he now? I'm sending Joy to pay him a fucking visit!" Tayana demanded unlocking her phone.

Yolan pulled Tayana's phone from her hand and held it between hers. "Tay, stop, he's not worth the time or effort it would take to find him. Besides, he packed up and left town shortly after I left him, might have had something to do with the nightly texts with pictures of my gun I sent him but I can't be 100% sure," Yolan admitted, smiling a little even though tears from that bitter memory rolled down her face.

"Damn, Yo, I don't know who's more gangster with that kind of shit, you or Whisper, but I have to ask what all of that has to do with Ryan?" Monet asked, passing her the box of tissues from the end table.

"Because he is just like Deon, successful, charming, knows all the right things to say, handsome, a little cocky. I refuse to let another man make me feel the way Deon did," she explained looking hopeless and pitiful.

"But he's not Deon! He's Ryan!" Both Tayana and Monet said at the same time, they looked over at each other and started laughing.

"Great minds," they said in unison.

"I don't care, he's a Buppie and down deep he will always see me as less than him. I have worked my ass off to be on top of my industry and for someone like him it will never be enough," Yolan argued, still licking her wounds from the past.

"Yo, how do you even know that? You are making Ryan pay for Deon's sins and it's not right. Hell, using your logic I should have never given Jazz a second glance after Thirst's double-crossing ass," Tayana reasoned looking over at Monet for back up.

"She's right, Yo and just like Whisper, the baddest females in the game got your back along with Jazz's crew, so if he turns out to be a snake ass individual we will end his ass, slow and painful, the torture I have in mind? It would take him days to die," Monet stated with an evil grin, her eyebrow arched in thought.

"Monet! Can she at least start dating him *before* you torture and kill him? Damn!" Tayana said, looking over at Monet shaking her head and laughing.

"I love and appreciate you both, and I hear what y'all are saying, but I honestly don't know if I'm ready to step into that arena again," Yolan admitted doubtfully, grabbing Monet's glass of sparkling water and drinking it all.

"Shit, Yo, with all that moaning and groaning you were doing when I got here earlier? You ready girl, beyond ready to climb that tree!" Tayana teased, laughing again.

Monet sat up looking over at Yolan with an evil glare as she got up to pour herself more sparkling water and brought back a glass for Yolan too.

"Damn... was she calling out too, Whisper?" Monet asked, laughing along with Tayana.

"Chile, if I would have given her a few more minutes she would have been!" Tayana answered reaching over and taking the glass of water Monet just poured for herself and winked at her.

Monet glared at them both before storming back to the kitchen grabbing another glass and the entire bottle of sparkling water and setting both on the table.

"Okay, I will admit I'm attracted to him, very attracted to him. The man's kisses do something to all my common sense, but I don't think that's enough to throw caution to the wind," Yolan said sitting back looking back and forth between both her sister/friends.

"It's enough to at least try to get to know the man and let him get to know you too, the real you, not the public perfectionist, Yolan Belle," Monet argued, pouring water into a third glass.

"Maybe. I'll think about it. Now onto a more important subject, did I see you bring in the ingredients for eggplant parmesan and if so what time are you cooking it? I am freaking starving!" Yolan asked, laying her head on Monet's shoulder, batting her eyes up at her.

"Greedy ass drama queen," Monet snapped, pushing Yolan's head off her shoulder.

———

"Hello?" Ryan answered his voice low and gravelly, like he had been sleeping, later on that night when she called.

Yolan looked over at the clock on her nightstand, it was 12:45a.m., she didn't stop to think that maybe he wasn't the night owl she was. She, Tayana, and Monet had dinner together and watched a couple of movies before they both called it a night and left.

That was about an hour ago and after a cold shower to calm her wayward thoughts, to no avail, she dialed his number.

"I'm so sorry, did I wake you up? Damn it is pretty late, just, um, call me tomorrow," Yolan rushed to get off the phone, embarrassed.

"Yolan?" he called her name sounding more alert.

"Yeah, it's me but like I said I didn't mean to wake you up, why don't you call me tomorrow after work?" she suggested fidgeting nervously.

"It's already tomorrow and it's Saturday. I'm not working today, I needed some time off. Anyway, what's up? Everything okay?" he asked, yawning.

She could hear him moving around in his bed. The images that popped into her head were not helping her cause. "Um, yeah, everything is fine, I was just calling to say… to say I'm sorry for acting so—" she paused not knowing how to phrase how she'd been acting towards him.

"Hot and cold? Evil? Standoffish?" Ryan suggested completing her sentence with a chuckle. "I could continue with more adjectives, but I believe you get the picture."

"I'm sure you could, and I'm sorry for being all of the

adjectives you did use and the ones you didn't use," Yolan quietly admitted, glad he couldn't see her blushing uncomfortably.

"Apology accepted, is that the only reason you called?" he asked curiously.

"No, I was wondering if you would like to meet me for dinner sometime soon? You pick the day, time, and restaurant and just let me know when? My treat," she asked, hugging one of her pillows to her, afraid she might be too late in offering the olive branch.

"Let me check my schedule and I'll let you know when we will be getting together again," Ryan stated in the stern voice that gave her chills. "Until then I better not have to hunt your ass down again or you will feel my wrath, understand?" he asked, his voice deep and low.

"Yes, Ryan, I understand, and I'll talk to you then," Yolan answered, silently screaming at herself for being so stupid knowing she blew it with him.

"We'll talk soon, goodnight, Yolan," he answered, his voice took on a sexy tone that traveled up her spine, giving her chills.

"Goodnight, Ryan, sweet dreams," she replied, crossing her legs tight as she began to throb.

She held the phone to her ear until she heard him hang up and tossed her phone on the bed before screaming into her pillow in frustration. Why was apologizing so damn difficult!

Chapter 6

Two months later

"I still say I won that last round," Ryan stated holding the door open for Yolan as they entered BBQ Bill's to grab something to eat after playing miniature golf.

They had gone out every other day for the past two months. Really getting to know Yolan had been the most fun he'd had in an exceptionally long time. He knew he was driving her crazy by not touching her the way she wanted to be touched, but that was on purpose. Yes, he gave her the sweet goodnight kisses and a few pats on the ass when she stepped too far out of line but other than that, nothing. It was all part of his payback for her playing cat and mouse with him for so long. In his eyes, bad behavior was never supposed to be rewarded. He wanted her ready to climb the walls and give in to his every whim and he could tell, by the hostile looks she had been throwing his way all night while they were playing miniature golf, she was almost there.

"Keep telling yourself that, sore loser," she quipped, looking up at the menu.

He stepped up behind her with his hands on her hips and leaned down and kissed her softly on the neck. "Am I really? Am I really a sore loser, Yolan, or are you are just hot and bothered about something else?" he whispered in her ear, dragging his tongue around the edge of it.

When she leaned back against him and moaned, he stepped to the side and smiled down at her. "I'm thinking we should get two entrees and different sides to share," he told her and moved forward to place their order while fighting back a wicked grin.

"I still say you're a sore loser," Yolan stated when they settled down at the table he chose at the very back of the restaurant.

"Me, a sore loser? Did you or did you not slam down your putter so hard it broke when I won by one stroke in the second game we played?" Ryan demanded, poking his straw through the plastic lid of his sweet tea, taking a healthy drink, smiling over at her expectantly.

"Well, yeah, but hey, I still paid my debt." Yolan blushed and looked over at him smiling.

He hid his smile behind his napkin as he remembered how she leaned in to give him a kiss and he gave her a quick, closed-lipped peck on the lips and winked before going back to playing golf. With amusement he caught her hard glare and how she held her club in her tight grip out of the corner of his eye before she stepped up to take her turn, he could tell she was suffering bad.

"Mmm, yes you did, which is why I say you cheated to win that last round," he argued leaning forward with his elbows on the table, his eyes shining as he looked at her across the table.

"No, I didn't! I won the last round fair and square and I aim to collect my prize." Yolan gloated over at him, leaning forward too, his eyes lowered to her cleavage for a brief moment then moved back to her face.

His bottom lip was caught between his teeth as his wayward thoughts began to surface, she smiled sweetly at him. "What were the terms again?" Ryan asked, frowning as if he was trying but didn't remember.

"Don't even try it, you agreed to the terms! Best two out of three, the loser owes the winner dinner and one bonus prize of the winner's choosing," Yolan quoted taking a bite of potato salad before smiling at him again.

"Oh yeah that's right," Ryan said quickly, snapping his fingers as if he suddenly remembered. His eyes once again traveled to her cleavage, his tongue peeked out of the corner of his mouth as he wet his bottom lip, fuck he wanted to kiss her there.

"Whatever, Ryan. Anyway I won, so I get dinner *and* a bonus of my choosing," Yolan bragged, taking a bite of macaroni and cheese from his plate, he took a piece of brisket from hers.

"So, what will you choose? Knowing you, something practical and boring," Ryan said, rolling his eyes feigning annoyance. He looked down at her feet wrapped in low, open-toe sandals, her soft, moisturized legs that gave off the scent of coconut oil as she moved.

He watched curiously as Yolan dipped her finger in the BBQ sauce on her plate and licked it slowly to taste it. Before sucking slowly from her fingertip, while looking up at the ceiling, as if she was thinking, but didn't answer his question.

"I'm waiting, Yolan," he warned and looked at her sternly after she was still quiet several seconds later.

She sighed, picked up a piece of hot link from his plate with her fork and took a small bite. Her tongue darted out and cleaned a drop of sauce from the corner of her mouth as she moaned, closing her eyes in bliss at the taste.

"Damn, that is so good, I can imagine only one thing that would taste even better," Yolan moaned, opening her eyes and staring over at him, pointedly. She sat back in her chair, crossing her legs, the hem of her light-peach slip dress slid up a little giving him a view of her upper thigh.

Ryan dragged his gaze up her body and noticed the sparkle of the glitter body mist she had sprayed on all of her skin not hidden by her clothes. The look that skirted across her face told him she could tell she was getting under his skin a little bit and she winked, smiling seductively when their eyes met again.

Ryan sat back in his chair, his fork paused in mid-air on the way to his mouth as he blinked over at her. She had no idea she was beginning to play an extremely dangerous game she had no way of winning and he felt his self-control slipping. He dropped his hand in his lap to try and shield his reaction to her.

Yolan reached over and touched the side of his face, letting her fingernails drag through his soft beard. "Have I told you how handsome you look today? I mean you always look handsome, but seeing you in regular old jeans instead of slacks, being able to see the shape of your legs has got me feeling some type of way," she whispered, still playing in his beard.

"You might want to stop playing with me, Yolan," he told her and dropped his fork back on his plate, trying to ignore her teasing, and reached over pinching a piece of brisket off her plate. Before he could get it to his mouth, she stopped his hand and led it to her mouth, lightly taking the bite of brisket from between his fingertips with her teeth and sucked the sauce from his fingers.

Ryan gently pulled his fingers from her warm mouth, shifting uncomfortably in his seat as he grew harder. He knew, right then, they needed to leave and they needed to do it sooner rather than later, he was at his breaking point.

"Dinner's over," he announced and signaled for their waitress, after asking for two takeout boxes and the check he refocused his attention on Yolan. "Let me tell you something, Yolan, playing with me is like playing with fire and while it might be fun at the moment, you might want to ask yourself if you really want to feel the burn the way I'm capable of delivering it," he warned with a menacing look, readjusting his erection, trying to think straight.

"What's wrong, Ryan? Did it just dawn on you that you're not a loser after all, but simply a second-place winner?" Yolan asked as he handed the waitress his card, never taking his eyes off of her. She sat across from him, smiling innocently, silently finishing her lemonade, pulling out her phone.

The waitress came back with his card and his receipt to sign and quickly boxed up their food and bid them a good night as she rushed away from them and the sexual tension swirling around them.

"No, Yolan. What's wrong with me is you playing your little game and having no idea of what I'm capable of," he told her, still looking intense. It was taking everything in his power not to snatch her out of her chair and take her over his knee right in the middle of the damn restaurant for messing with him.

"Shit, at this point you could pull up in a parking lot and that would be cool with me," she quipped, staring over at him pointedly. Her eyes were relaying a very clear message of what she not only wanted but needed.

"Let your driver know he can come pick you up, our evening is at its end," Ryan ordered, his already deep voice sounded like a growl as he stared over at her with his eyes narrowed. He had noticed that no matter where they went, Yolan's car and driver were parked nearby, at first it was a little unsettling but now he had gotten used to it.

"I already texted him a few minutes ago, and if it's all right with you, I asked him to drive us to your house, one of my people will drive your car over later," Yolan informed him, grabbing her purse and standing.

"That won't be necessary," Ryan told her and stood up, pulling his shirt down and trying to cover his erection that was pressing against the zipper of his jeans. When he saw it wasn't going to work, he walked closely behind Yolan, he smacked her on the ass hard enough to make it sting before grabbing her by the waist and steering her out of the restaurant, his dick hard and ready, pressed against her back.

Ryan remained behind her with his front pressed tightly against her back. He could tell from the way she subtly moved her hips against him she was ready to take their mutual attraction to the next level. When he saw her car pull up, he stepped to the side and opened the door before her driver could even exit the vehicle, and ushered her inside. When she reached out to take him with her, he backed away out of her reach.

"Good night, Yolan, it was fun." Was all he said before closing the car door and knocking on the top of it to let her driver know they could leave.

The look of surprise mixed with disbelief on her face as her car pulled away from the curb was priceless. Yolan had no idea who she was dealing with, but he was hoping this made one thing abundantly clear, she may be running things at Royalty but when it came to the pace of their relationship, he was in charge.

'Good morning, Yolan, I hope you slept as well as I did.' Was the text Yolan woke up to from Ryan the following morning, after sleeping for only about two hours. She had been so sure Ryan was going to address her needs when they left the restaurant that it floored her when he walked her to her car and sent her

on her way with a smug smile. She tossed and turned due to her sexual frustration all night long.

"Arghh! God, he makes me sick!" Yolan screamed, kicking and beating her fists on her bed in frustration before finally getting up and stomping off to the shower with her body still screaming for the release only Ryan could provide.

"Girl, why do you look like you're about to kill somebody?" Monet asked looking up from the magazine she was thumbing through when Yolan walked into Jaidyn and Khyrs' salon, *Ghetto Star* two hours later. She and Monet were going to lunch after getting their hair done at her request. She had to keep herself busy and things were dead at the office at the moment due to the continued construction for security. They weren't losing any money, but they had decided to postpone any new client appointments until the following week when the final touches would be done.

Yolan rolled her eyes and flopped down in Jaidyn's chair, across from Monet who was in Khyrs' chair getting her hair flat ironed straight, and sighed. "Ryan Devoe is a heartless sadist, that's why," she mumbled, while pulling her phone out of her purse to see if he said anything else after she texted him good morning back and she was glad he slept well. When she saw the winky face emoji he sent back she felt her blood begin to boil. "Oh, hell no!" she snapped and tossed her phone back into her bag.

"Yo, what the hell are you talking about now?" Monet asked, as Jaidyn wrapped the protective cape around Yolan, shaking her head. Ever since Tayana and Monet had encouraged her to face her fears and give Ryan a chance, Yolan was always complaining about something he did or said.

"Yeah, what did you do to the poor man now?" Jaidyn asked picking up a wide tooth comb and combing through Yolan's hair. She was only getting her hair styled since she had a wash and deep condition four days before, she mainly came to the salon to hang out with the ladies and burn off some sexual energy before she and Monet went to lunch to discuss the double baby shower for Tayana and Asia.

"Why do you naturally assume I did something to him, Jaidyn?" Yolan asked, glaring at Jaidyn through the mirror in front of her, now was not the time for her and Monet's foolishness.

"Tell me you didn't do something and before you do, remember who you're talking to," Jaidyn said parting her hair and adding clips to keep it divided. "We know you better than anybody," Jaidyn reminded her with a shit eating grin.

Yolan looked at all three ladies, her glare was rebellious. "You guys don't understand, he has gone from snatching me and kissing me and touching me like his life depended on it to treating me like his fucking cousin," Yolan explained, folding her arms and sitting back with a pout.

Monet, Khyrs and Jaidyn all exchanged looks before all three women started laughing.

"As he should! Hell, I can't say I blame the man, he's probably tired of going home with blue balls and decided to slow things down until he's sure you're done playing with his emotions," Monet said knowingly when they stopped laughing.

"What the hell ever, Mo. No matter what he's feeling, what he did to me last night was just plain evil," Yolan snapped, still pouting and shooting daggers at Khyrs and Jaidyn but saving her most hostile look for Monet.

The trio exchanged looks again and smirked. "Okay, Yo, what did he do?" Khyrs asked, pausing with the flat iron in her hand.

"Nothing! That's what! Last night I decided to take matters into my own hands and tease him while we at dinner. I messed with him so bad the man cut dinner short and walked me out of the restaurant. Y'all the man was ready, you know what I mean?" Yolan told them remembering how Ryan's rock-hard erection was pressed against her back as they waited for Troop.

"And?" Monet asked, waving her hands in a circular motion encouraging Yolan to continue talking.

"And that's it! The bastard helped me into my car and closed the door," Yolan told them, feeling herself getting sexually frustrated all over again just thinking about it .

All three ladies started laughing again, this time so hard they didn't stop for several minutes.

"I am really beginning to like this Ryan dude," Jaidyn quipped, looking at Yolan with amusement dancing in her eyes.

"I agree, he sounds like a keeper, Yo," Monet said and nodded, fighting to keep the smile off of her face.

"You *cannot* be serious; did you not hear what I said he did to me?" Yolan snapped, looking ready to kill all three of them.

"Yes, I heard every word you said and I still say, *Bravo Ryan*. Your evil ass is always trying to control something, sometimes you're even worse than Whisper, Yo. I'm glad he's not letting you run all over him because, be honest, if he did you would just get bored and lose interest with a quickness," Monet said, taking the mirror from Khyrs so she could see the back of her head now that her hair was finished.

"That's not true, Mo. What he did was totally wrong, and you know it," Yolan argued, hating the fact the ladies were siding with Ryan and not her.

"No, what *you* did was totally wrong, Yo. You have been playing with this man's emotions for a minute and instead of asking him why he wasn't as affectionate towards you, you played with them again, and while you were out to dinner no less. In all of your time pouting and feeling shortchanged, have you stopped to think for a second how embarrassing that might have been for him last night? I mean you know the man wants you and you know he wants you bad so I can only imagine what state he must have been in from you *'messing with him'*," Monet admonished.

"Look, Yo, it's like this, sometimes it's okay to let a man lead and in matters of the heart I really think they should. Now, I'm not saying let a man take advantage or run over you and you should just take it, or anything like that. But I am saying let the man be the man and if he is a good one, like we all believe and you know down deep Ryan is, you will be okay, just stop trying to control every damn thing and let this thing play out naturally," Monet told her, with a smile.

Yolan wanted so badly to protest but she knew Monet was right. She needed to open the lines of communication and really give Ryan a chance, but before any of that she needed to apologize for last night.

"Fine, Monet, as much as I hate to admit it you're right, Heffa. But I will say this, you need to follow your own advice and stop running from Diamond's ass too."

"Hello, Yolan, you asked that I call when I had a moment to talk?" Ryan asked when Yolan answered her phone later that same evening. He had made it a point to keep his text messages short and sweet, mostly limited to two or three word answers all day. Yes, they needed to talk but talking via text just wasn't going to cut it.

He heard her take a deep breath before speaking. "Ryan, I just wanted to say I was sorry for the way I behaved last night, and I wanted to ask you something too," she said, her voice was soft as if she was lying down or he woke her up.

Even though he was still a little upset with her, his mind went to images of Yolan in lacy lingerie or nothing at all, lying in the middle of a bed covered in pillows and silk, her smooth skin glowing in candlelight.

"I appreciate the apology, Yolan. It tells me you had time to think about everything that transpired last night and you will do anything to ensure nothing like that will happen again," he said, more than a little surprised she came around and admitted her wrongdoing so quickly.

"I have and it won't. What I did was uncalled for and more than a little selfish, so again I apologize, do you think we can move past it and continue forward from here?" she asked cautiously.

Ryan's eyes widened even more in surprise, this calm and accommodating woman was not the Yolan he was used to.

"I believe we can. If you don't already have plans we can meet for dinner tomorrow," he told her with a smile on his face. This softer side of Yolan was showing him he had a lot more to learn about her and he was anxious to start peeling back the layers to see what he would find.

She felt her heart leap happily when she saw him walking towards the table she had been seated at in the back of the restaurant. It had only been two days since she saw him last, but she had actually missed him more than she ever realized when she saw him.

"Good evening, Yolan, you look even more breathtaking than usual tonight," he said as he moved over to her and held out his hand when he reached the table. Yolan immediately took it without question and smiled brightly when he helped her to her feet and hugged her to him before kissing her softly on the lips.

"Thank you, Ryan, you're looking pretty good yourself this evening," she said when he let her go and sat down in the seat across from her. Yolan sat back down in her own chair and took a sip of her ginger ale.

"So tell me, Yolan, you said you were sorry but you didn't exactly go into detail what you were sorry for," he stated opening the menu that was next to his plate on the table.

"Seriously, Ryan?" Yolan sighed and took another sip of her drink, she should have known he wasn't going to make things easy for her to be forgiven. "You know what I did and why I'm sorry," she argued.

Ryan sat back closing the menu, looking over at her. His eyes were narrow and piercing. "And I believe I asked you to clarify exactly what you're apologizing for in detail, so I know we are on the same page. I won't ask again, Yolan," he told her before pausing and leaning over to talk to their server to order a drink.

When he was finished, his eyes focused back onto her face expectantly. Something about his intense gaze and no-nonsense demeanor was beginning to turn her on, causing her to squirm in her chair.

"Yolan, perhaps we decided to meet again too soon," Ryan said and moved in his chair as if he was going to stand to leave.

"Ryan, calm down, I was just getting my thoughts together," Yolan reasoned reaching out and touching his arm. "For clarification I was apologizing for being overly sexual at dinner the other night and trying to force you to move at my pace instead of your own."

Ryan nodded taking a swallow of the drink their server just set in front of him. "I appreciate that, Yolan and believe me when I say going at my pace will be a benefit to us both, the heightened sense of want that comes from anticipation is its own aphrodisiac.

"When I finally decide it's time to succumb to our mutual attraction, wants and desires, you will see it was well worth the wait," Ryan promised returning his attention to his menu. "Now then, did you decide what you wanted to have or would you like for me to order for us both?"

"Um, why don't you order for us both since I have never been here before," Yolan answered biting the inside of her cheek to suppress the moan of frustration as a pressing question clawed at her throat to be heard. Waiting was all well and good but was she really supposed to be satisfied with just chaste good night kisses and limited physical affection until that time came? She was already damn near climbing the walls as it was, he had to know that was absolute torture and the devious smile now playing on his face when he looked at her again told her that was exactly what he was aiming for.

"I have to admit I didn't think I was going to like that movie, but it was actually pretty good," Yolan told Ryan two weeks later as they walked hand in hand towards the small bistro near the movie theater, he had chosen for dinner. They were back to seeing each other every day and Ryan had even showed up at her office to take her out to lunch a few times.

Since the night of miniature golf, Yolan was a little bit more subdued, she was still her *take no prisoners* business minded self but when she was with him, she let him lead. Instead of saying they were going to do this or that, she would suggest it or ask his opinion on it before making concrete plans. All of their physical contact of late was initiated by him, from simple kisses to hand holding, she followed his cues and she had no idea how much that turned him on.

"I'm glad you liked it, Yolan, I figured you would. Listen, I know I suggested we go grab a bite to eat after the movie, but I was thinking we could do something else instead," he said, pulling her into a darkened doorway of a clothing shop that was closed for the night.

He pressed her up against the glass with his body, grabbing her by the chin and forced his tongue in her mouth, she moaned deep in her chest and went up on the tips of her toes to put her arms around his neck. Ryan reached down, grabbing her by her ass, and lifted her off of her feet as he pinned her even tighter between his body and the glass display window behind her.

His tongue plunged in and out of her mouth, coaxing hers to come out and join the fun. Yolan wrapped her legs around his waist and gripped his shoulders tight as his strong, massive hands kneaded her behind and moved her aggressively against his growing erection.

Ryan moved one hand from her ass to the zipper on her shirt and dragged it down slowly, tearing his lips from hers, he dragged his tongue down her neckline into her cleavage causing her to twitch and pant with want.

"We can do whatever you want to do, Ryan, just please, for the love of God, don't stop what you're doing right now," Yolan moaned, gripping his shoulders and moving against his erection as much as being pinned by his body would allow.

Ryan lifted his head and looked down at her, her eyes were shining with desire as her chest heaved with her panted breathing giving him an even better look into her cleavage.

"Mmm, sounds like a plan. Call your driver and tell him I got you covered, he can take the rest of the night off," he ordered, dropping kisses on her neck. He felt her stiffen at once and lifted his head.

"Something wrong, Yolan?" he asked, his voice low and demanding as he looked at her again. She was biting her bottom lip nervously; he could tell she wanted to say something contrary to what he requested.

"Ryan, I-I can't do that," she finally pushed out breathlessly, her eyes dancing with regret and apology.

Ryan took a step back and helped her stand back on her feet. "Are you saying you don't want to spend the night with me, Yolan?" he asked her carefully, feeling a little annoyed by her refusal.

"No, no I'm not saying that at all, it's just—" she trailed off and looked down at the ground. He immediately lifted her chin and made her look at him again.

"It's just what, Yolan?" Ryan asked, running his thumb softly across her face as he looked at her. She seemed so conflicted and vulnerable, and he couldn't understand why.

"Ryan, there is so much about me I want you to know, but I really can't talk about yet. But for tonight, just so this night can continue, can you allow me this one concession and have my driver take us to your place? I will make sure your car gets taken there as well," Yolan said in a rush, looking up at him and shifting her weight from side to side nervously. "Besides, with you not having to keep your eyes on the road, you can keep them and your hands on me instead," she suggested with a sultry smile, dragging the zipper down on her shirt even further.

Ryan felt his dick jump in anticipation at the thought of getting Yolan to his house and completely out of her clothes and under his control. He could tell her request was one made out of need and not to be defiant and knowing he was willing to compromise.

"Make that call and tell him to hurry the hell up," Ryan growled, pressing her against the glass again as he lowered his mouth onto hers.

As soon as they crossed the threshold into Ryan's house, he dropped to his knees and pulled her into his arms. Even on his knees he was several inches taller than her, his mouth came down on hers forcefully, his tongue immediately in her mouth.

He grabbed the back of her head and drove his tongue deeper to the back of her mouth causing their teeth to clash. Yolan wrapped her arms around his neck and kissed him back with the same fervor.

He tore his mouth from hers, breathing hard and dropped kisses on the side of her face and down her neck. His hands ran up her legs softly as she moaned, marveling at his touch. His hands climbed higher as his head moved lower, his soft lips were on her shoulders.

Ryan pulled her top up and over her head quickly, tossing it behind him and continued his mouth's journey south. Yolan's breasts stood high and proud in her half cup lace bra, her erect nipples poked forward against the material beckoning to him.

He leaned forward, kissing her on the top of each breast as he reached behind her and unfastened her bra. Her ample breasts sprang free into his waiting hands, he massaged them both and squeezed the nipples between his thumb and forefinger, causing shock waves to ricochet through her body as her nipples grew even harder.

Yolan's breath came out in wanting pants as he gripped her breasts tightly together flicking his tongue across both nipples before sucking them each in turn.

"Shit, Ryan your mouth feels so good!" She hissed fighting to keep standing, her legs were beginning to shake as her pussy grew wetter and wetter.

He made himself at home sucking and licking her breasts, he kissed every part of them even the underside and went right back to the nipples like they were made just for him.

Yolan's middle pulsed and throbbed screaming for attention too, as he left a hickey between her breasts before he sat back on his heels, licking his lips looking at her standing in front of him in Capri length leggings and her low heeled sandals, like every one of his fantasies come to life. He dragged his hands down her sides and moved them into the waistband of her leggings pushing them down over her hips and thighs to her ankles before he helped her out of her shoes and tossed the leggings aside to join her discarded shirt.

"Come here," he commanded with a husky whisper, as his hungry eyes traveled up and down her body, greedily taking in her naked breasts and lace underwear.

Yolan moved forward and dropped onto his lap, her legs straddled on either side of his hips. Ryan's erection pressed against her lace covered mound as she grabbed him by his collar and kissed him as deeply as he had kissed her. She wasted no time getting him out of his shirt and dropping kisses all over his bare, muscular chest.

Her hips ground against him, the friction caused by her thong and his jeans made her even wetter and the subtle scent of her arousal and coconut body cream perfumed the air around them.

"Shit! Yolan, you're killing me. Baby, slow down!" Ryan swore as she kissed his neck and lifted off of his lap just enough to whisper in his ear.

"But what a way to go," she chuckled and flicked her tongue around his ear to drive him even crazier.

Ryan let out a low growl and surged to his feet, his hands gripping Yolan by the ass as he stood. He walked her over to the first chair he could see in his aroused state, he pulled a condom from his wallet, let his pants fall, sat down and rolled it on his long, hard erection and sat her down on the tip of it.

Yolan's eyes opened wide as he filled her completely, stretching her walls to capacity, until the tip of his dick was at the back of her pussy twitching deep inside of her.

"Holy shit, Ryan," Yolan panted, her hands were on his shoulders, her nails leaving crescent shaped indentations in his skin.

He grabbed her by the waist and began to move her up and down on his dick. His movements were slow and deliberate at first to let her get used to his girth, once her thighs relaxed and she began to move her hips in time with his thrusts, he lifted her higher driving deeper into her every time their middles met.

"Oh my fucking God, Yolan! How is it possible for you to feel this fucking good! Damn, Baby, damn, this pussy is amazing!" he shouted against her ear as his aggressive strokes continued. His head dipped and he captured one of her bouncing breasts in his mouth sucking hard on the nipple.

Yolan threw her head back fighting the urge to give in to the sensation overload and the orgasm already rising inside of her.

Ryan felt her pulsing around him beginning to squeeze tight, he lifted her off of his lap and laid her on the floor spreading her legs wide and dove back in, he was so deep inside of her, he couldn't tell where he ended, and she began.

Yolan clawed at his back and arms as the first waves hit her. "Ryan! Goddamn! No! Not yet! Please not yet!" she yelled as she pulsed and vibrated around his erection, her juice spilled out wetting the floor beneath her.

Ryan stroked slowly and held her tight as she continued to come, when her body stilled, he lightly kissed her forehead, her eyelids, her nose, and her lips, still resting inside of her.

She struggled to open her eyes briefly because, like the rest of her body, her eyelids felt heavy. When she finally did, he was smiling down at her with that slow, sexy smile of his.

"You all right?" he asked, kissing her again, he made his dick jump inside of her, causing her to arch off of the floor.

"Damn Ry, I think I'm still coming," she murmured as she felt her body begin to shake again.

"Damn, if a quickie earns me a nickname, I wonder what stroking you all night will get me," Ryan mused softly as he began moving slowly inside of her again.

Yolan bit her bottom lip and grabbed him around the waist as he began to ride her body into bliss once again.

Candlelight and raindrops.

In her mind, this moment couldn't have been more perfect if she had ordered it personally.

Ryan walked in holding two glasses and a bottle of chilled champagne, as she sat in the huge black papasan chair in front of the large picture window in his bedroom watching the raindrops hit the glass. She was completely naked, her body was still vibrating from the wild sex they had had, basically in Ryan's entry way.

Yolan watched him as he moved closer to her, her eyes traveled down his frame, admiring him from his long muscular legs to his broad chest and shoulders to his handsome face and honey brown eyes.

Ryan was wonderful to look at with his clothes on but a true sight to behold when he was naked. He made her mouth water, she felt herself getting wet all over again as her middle jumped and thumped.

"Like what you see?" he asked, setting the glasses on the bedside table and popping the cork on the champagne.

Yolan stretched leisurely and nodded as she stood up and walked over to him.

She took the bottle from him after he poured them each a glass full of champagne and guided him in front of the chair she just vacated.

He looked down at her, a sexy ass smile plastered on his face, his eyes low and shining. "So, what's up?" he asked, spreading his arms out to his sides.

Yolan set the bottle closer to the chair and window and lightly placed her hands on his chest and pushed him backward, so he landed in the chair.

"It's like that, huh?" he asked, looking down at her through hooded eyes.

Still silent, Yolan grabbed both glasses of champagne and handed him one and the universal remote she assumed was hooked to the hidden speakers in each corner of the room.

"What are you up to?" he asked, his dick already beginning to rise, as he turned on his sound system and Prince's song *"Do Me Baby"* immediately filled the room, drowning out the sound of raindrops.

Yolan took a drink of her champagne and smiled at him, desire rising up in her once again. "Watch," she whispered to him leaning forward until her lips could touch his, her tongue lightly licked his bottom lip tasting the champagne he just drank.

Yolan stood back up and started to move to the music, her hips moved from side to side. She ran her hands slowly over her body cupping her breasts before moving her hands lower and spreading open her thighs.

Ryan watched her, fighting to appear in control but he was already almost at full attention.

When she bent over and continued to move her hands down her legs, spreading them wider and wider until she was in a forward split in front of him, Ryan drained his glass of champagne and quickly poured another one.

Yolan gyrated and rolled her body as she rode the floor, flashing him a full view of her Brazilian waxed box.

Ryan grabbed his erection and slowly moved his hand up

and down the length, his eyes even lower, he bit his bottom lip as he watched her dance.

Yolan pulled her legs together and got onto her knees reaching for her own champagne as she watched him grow even harder before her eyes.

"See something you like?" he quipped, raising his eyebrows at her.

"I'm not sure, I need to see how it tastes first," Yolan answered softly and began to crawl over to him.

When she reached him, she rose up on her knees and spread his legs apart, his hand was still moving slowly up and down his shaft. Yolan grabbed her glass and filled her mouth with the last of the cold champagne before leaning forward and running her tongue up his balls.

He stiffened, arching off the chair a little and hissed through his teeth as her tongue moved higher, the bubbles from the champagne tickling him as she went. Ryan dropped his hands to the sides of the chair and let her take over. Yolan had about a swallow of champagne still in her mouth when she reached the tip of his penis and took the head into her mouth with slow and steady suction. Ryan gripped the sides of the chair and arched his hips pushing his dick further into her mouth.

Yolan opened her mouth wider and allowed him to fuck her mouth, his moans grew louder, making her even wetter. She loved the taste of him on her tongue, the way the veins in his dick pulsated in her mouth, the sounds of unfiltered pleasure he was making.

She found herself wishing there was a way to fuck him and suck him at same time since her mouth gave him so much pleasure and the need to have him pounding inside her slithered up her spine and took over her thoughts.

She moved her head backwards slowly, regretfully, until he fell from her mouth.

Ryan threw his head back and let out a growl of frustration that immediately turned into a moan of pleasure as she positioned herself over him and her wet box slid all the way down his erection.

"Fucckk!" he hissed, closing his eyes as she began to move her hips, matching the movement she was making while in the splits on the floor. She pulled his head to hers and pushed her tongue deep in his mouth tonguing him down as she rose high and came all the way back down on him.

His massive hands grabbed her hips and held her tight, bringing her back down as he thrust his hips upwards to drive into her deeper.

She was stretched wide by the size of his invasion, the mixture of pleasure and pain his massiveness caused had her seeing stars and her body trembling.

"Ryan, damn what are you doing to me?" she sang and hit a high note as he went even deeper.

The chair began to creak and rock as they continued to slam into each other, their moans and cries were louder than the now raging thunderstorm outside and music playing in the room combined.

He bit her earlobe and pressed his mouth against her ear. "I can't get enough of you, my dick is hitting the bottom and I still want to go deeper! Fuck, Ny, fuck you got me so fucking hard right now it hurts!" Ryan's hands moved from her hips to her ass, he took a firm grip and repositioned her so instead of going in straight up and down, he was at an angle hitting her G-spot.

Yolan closed her eyes tight, leaned back and arching her body into a backbend, her hands braced on the carpeted floor as he pounded on.

"Goddamn, Baby," he hissed, surprised and turned on even more by how flexible she was at the same time. His fingers dug into her ass as he held her tighter and moved his hips from side to side to experience all she was offering him.

The chair suddenly tipped too far forward because of their aggressive movements, spilling them onto the floor, their connection never broke.

Ryan lifted her legs onto his shoulders and continued to ram into her, sweat poured off of them both as they continued to move, the craving to devour each other driving them recklessly towards the same goal.

Yolan bit his bicep to keep from screaming out loud as she was beginning to climb towards her euphoric end. Her orgasm started at the tips of her toes this time, the ringing in her ears sounded like someone struck a massive Tibetan singing bowl by her head.

The beautiful, haunting sound vibrated from deep within her as she soared higher, her calves spasmed, her thighs shook as his relentless strokes continued, the chill that shot up her spine and through her limbs caused her to tremble all over.

"Ryan! Holyfuckingshit! Holyfuckshit! Damn Baby Damnn!" she screamed at the top of her lungs, she gulped for air as she was pulled under the waves of passion by the weight of her completion.

Ryan's hips lifted high one last time before he slammed into her hard and erupted inside of her. "Goddamn, Ny! Your pussy got me weak, Baby, fuck!" he swore and collapsed on top of her.

She could feel their juices creating a puddle underneath her, as she tried to catch her breath. He held her close as they both continued to shake, eyes closed tight as the shivering of orgasmic pleasure continued.

Yolan felt tears rolling from her eyes backwards into her hair as he rocked her slowly bringing them both back down to earth.

"I have never felt anything like that in my life," she admitted quietly, quickly wiping away her tears.

He looked down at her and kissed her lips. "Me either, Ny, me either. I'm sure I pulled or dislocated something I just feel too damn good to care right now." He chuckled moving her hair, moist with sweat from her face, resting on his elbows above her. He leaned forward and kissed her lips softly.

"Ny? Why are you calling me that?" Yolan asked, touching his face when they broke apart again, smiling up at him curiously.

"I told you I wanted to find a nickname that only I called you, and in my opinion your first name Nyiesha fits you so much more than Yolan does," he stated placing random kisses on her face, running his fingers through her hair.

"Still in Love" by Troop filled the room and to her surprise he started to sing it, his sex hazed eyes never left hers as he sang.

Yolan felt something beyond orgasmic contentment move through her and shook from the realization, she had done more than just catch feelings for Ryan, she had messed around and fallen in love. Shit.

"You do realize this will be our first weekend apart in I don't know how long, right?" Ryan teased leaning over and kissing Yolan who was cooking them breakfast in a tank top and boy shorts.

She didn't wear many clothes when she was over his house, it was only a matter of time before he relieved her of them anyway. She and the entire crew were going to Jazz and Tayana's place in Galveston for a girl's weekend, leaving Jazz and the men of The Firm in charge.

"Yes, Ryan I am aware of that fact, what's your point?"

she asked, pouring Ryan a glass of orange juice and handing it to him before she put all the food she cooked into serving dishes and moved them to the kitchen table.

"My point is I have no idea what I'm going to do with an entire two days without you, Ny," he admitted putting food on a plate and handing it to her, before dishing himself up a bigger portion.

"Ryan, it's one weekend and I only spend the night on Fridays and Saturdays so what are you even talking about 'two entire days'?" Yolan asked, mixing her grits and scrambled eggs together.

"Even the days you don't stay the night we still see each other and again I want to go on the record to say that is so damn nasty!" he said with his face twisted referring to her grits and eggs.

"And I want you to please refer to our previous conversation about the subject of my eating habits and return to your own damn plate!" Yolan snapped, smiling and taking a bite of her food.

"Ugh! I guess as perfect as you are, you had to have at least one flaw, huh?" Ryan asked, taking a bite of his own food.

"I am nowhere near perfect, Ryan, you just like my gymnastic skills." Yolan smiled over at him wickedly and winked.

"Shit, like? Ny, I love, love, love your gymnastics skills!" Ryan said loudly, winking back. He reached over and pulled her chair closer to his and reached down taking her leg and putting it across his lap and went back to eating his food with one hand, while his other hand was softly stroking her soft skin on the inside of her thigh, causing her to squirm.

"Ryan, you know I have to meet Monet at my place this afternoon so we can head up to Tay's before it gets dark," Yolan stated as his fingers moved up her thigh.

"Yeah and? We're eating breakfast together before you go, what's wrong with that?" he asked with a maddening look on his face, like he wasn't in the process of driving her wild with want.

"Whatever, Ryan, you know what you're doing, you don't play fair." Yolan glared over at him, her eyes narrowed as his hand moved higher touching the hem of her shorts.

"I have no idea what you're talking about," he said softly taking his last bite of food, Yolan's food was virtually untouched and growing cold as his finger pushed into her warm, wet, center.

She dropped her fork and gripped the table as his finger woke up her clit by touching it lightly. "Ryan, you know you ain't right." Yolan sighed sitting back in her chair giving him better access. His finger moved in and out of her making her wetter, she was about to climb in his lap when his phone rang.

He pulled it out of his pocket and placed it face up on the table between them, his finger still moving inside of her, when he saw who it was, he rolled his eyes in irritation.

"Fuck! I got to take this." He removed his now soaking wet finger from her and licked it dry, grinning wickedly at her surprised look as he left the kitchen and went into his office closing the door behind him.

Yolan cleared the table and loaded the dishes in the dish-washer to expel the sexual energy coursing through her body, she never did finish her breakfast.

When he didn't come back into the living room after thirty minutes, she went into his room to grab her clothes and take a shower while he worked.

Her eyes were closed and she was humming to the music she set to play in the bathroom as the sprays rained down on her body, refreshing, but still not enough to extinguish the fire Ryan had started. The thought of leaving with an orgasm in escrow had her ready to scream.

Massive hands suddenly grabbed her thighs jerking her from her thoughts, her eyes opened in surprise, Ryan was lying down on his back in the shower, staring up at her.

"Are you crazy? You scared the hell out of me!" she snapped reaching over and turning down the spray of water from the top nozzle so he didn't drown.

He gripped her legs tighter and pulled her forward until she bent her knees and her pussy was positioned over his face. Yolan grabbed the bars on either side of the shower as he brought his head up and buried his face between her thighs.

His tongue ran up the center of her pussy slowly and twirled around her clit before he began to suck on it softly. Yolan closed her eyes and moaned as his mouth made a meal out of her middle. The warm water from the shower trickled down on them reminding Yolan of rain.

His tongue moved inside her opening, and she allowed him to move her hips the way he wanted to continue his feast. She was on fire as she screamed out his name, holding on tight to the bars, vibrations from her middle shot through her as her juices rained down on Ryan's skilled tongue and mouth.

He moved his head and kissed the inside of both of her thighs and blew on her clit, causing her to shake even more. Her eyes were still closed tight as he brought his mouth back to her clit and sucked it harder.

"Oh my god, Ryan! Damn, Baby, damn! Please, please! Please! Don't ever stop!" she screamed, the entire bathroom was thick with steam.

When he could feel that she was seconds away from coming again, he sat up quickly and dropped her down on his erection and growled against her ear, "Come for me, Ny, come hard!" Yolan managed to move up and down on him twice before she exploded into a million pieces.

He grabbed her by the hips and fucked her through her orgasm until she was no longer thinking straight, spasming and pulsating around his dick, then and only then did he allow himself to come too and exploded deep inside of her.

———

"So, who is this then?" Yolan asked Ryan early afternoon the same day, pointing at an elegant older woman wearing her Sunday best. He caught her with his photo album when he came out after his real shower, so he was telling her about his family.

Monet was meeting her at the apartment at 3 o'clock so they could leave for the trip, so she had one hour left to spend with Ryan.

"That's my grandmother Katherine, everyone called her Grandma Kat, she passed away a year ago in December, two days after Christmas," he explained smiling at her picture in a loving way.

"I'm sorry, I didn't mean to bring up hurtful memories, we don't have to keep going," Yolan said, moving to close the album. She was sitting sideways with her legs across his lap, the album across hers.

"No, I want to talk to you about my family, Ny, I hope you will actually want to meet them some day," he said smiling down at her, kissing her softly. "It might also get you to talk about your family too."

"Maybe," she said quietly and thoughtfully. From what she saw, his entire family was successful and professional, what would they think about him bringing someone like her home? Yolan pushed the thought out of her mind and turned the page, her heart dropped as she stared at a picture of Ryan and Jazz locked in a homie hug, their hands in a fist bump.

She could tell they were both much younger than they were now, but it was definitely them. She pulled her eyes away and scanned the page seeing more pictures of them together at various ages. She looked up at him in question, unable to speak, her face was getting hot as she tried not to panic.

He looked down and broke out into a nostalgic smile pointing to the picture of them as teenagers, dressed alike.

"That's my cousin, Jazz, more like my brother honestly. We grew up together, he's the only one besides me who still lives here in Houston, the rest of the family is scattered through South Carolina now," Ryan told her, still smiling not realizing Yolan had literally stopped breathing.

She blinked trying to comprehend what he said, Jazz was his cousin? They grew up together like brothers! She could feel the walls closing in on her. "Um, do you– do you still s-s-see him often?" Yolan asked, trying to appear relaxed, when in reality her heart was pounding in her ears, her emotions were in a tangled mess.

"Not as often as we'd like, Jazz is on a different grind nowadays, he tap dances on the other side of the law if you know what I mean so I got to be careful when we hang out, but we still try to meet up for dinner or catch a game from time to time. Of course, he just got married not too long ago and they are having their first baby so he's spending a lot more time with his wife, her name's Whisper, can you believe that? Whisper. Since he met her, I told him her name is cool as shit, so unique until I met you, Nyiesha Marinna Yolan Belle, but she's cool people from what I hear though, perfect for Jazz," Ryan said smiling over at Yolan before his smile dropped looking over at her with concern.

She was pale and blinking rapidly, sweat gathered at her hairline. "I-I-I have to go, I um just remembered something I need to do before I leave for um…" Her mind went blank, she couldn't think of anything but getting the hell out of his house!

She jumped up and rushed to his bedroom grabbing her

overnight bag and texted Troop to meet her outside ASAP. It was like her nightmares were coming to life!

"Galveston, you're going to Galveston, Ny. Are you okay? You look like you're about to be sick. Do you need me to drive you home?" Ryan asked following behind her, looking alarmed.

"No, no I can't trust– I mean, I'm not ready, I mean– never mind, it's okay I texted Troop he will be here in a minute." Yolan was shaking all over from head to toe from fear and disbelief. Once he found out who she was to Jazz and Tayana, they were finished. She assumed he and Tayana never met, or he would have recognized her the day she walked into the office to meet with Yolan or vice versa, Tayana never forgot a face.

"What's going on, Ny? And since when do you stutter? And were you just about to say you can't trust me?" Ryan asked leaning against the doorframe of his room with his arms folded, eyes on her suspiciously.

"Nothing is wrong, Ryan. I just need to go, of course I trust you," she stated nervously shifting her weight from one foot to the other.

"Then message Troop and tell him I'm taking you home and to meet you there," Ryan challenged looking down at her, his eyes dark and demanding.

Yolan bit her bottom lip to keep from screaming at him and at herself for being so stupid. "I can't do that," she answered quietly looking down at her feet, her bare feet, she almost left without her shoes.

She quickly rushed past Ryan and grabbed her ballet slippers from under the couch, where they landed the night before when he scooped her up and carried her to his room.

"See? That's that shit, Ny! Why can't you?" Ryan asked with a frown, trying to understand what the hell was going on.

"Ryan there's a lot going on in my life right now– I mean

you are a part of my life but there's other– Forget it, you just don't, you will never–, because–" Yolan ran her hand through her hair, fighting to find the right words. He just wouldn't understand the reason why and she couldn't explain it and keep him in her life.

"Because you don't trust me. After all that has happened since our first date and that craziness, have I ever questioned you or doubted you? The fact you carry a gun with or on you at all times, the new armed security at Royalty, and let's not forget Troop, your armed driver who is never more than ten minutes away. And the elephant in the room, we have been dating for over four months now and I have never been to your house and yet I haven't said a word about any of it to you or anybody and now you stand here and tell me, less than an hour after climbing off of my face that you can't trust me?" Ryan asked looking over at her coldly, hurt swimming in his eyes too.

Yolan knew it was only a matter of time before she lost him anyway so why not just get it over with now? She reasoned with herself as her anxiety gave way to hurt, she took a deep breath still trembling, her stomach in anxious knots.

The words tasted so foul on her tongue before she pushed them out of her mouth. "No, I don't trust you, Ryan. I don't know if I ever will. I knew something like this would happen! I told you this would never work but you didn't listen!" Yolan snapped and stormed out of his house and into the backseat of her waiting car before he could stop her.

When Troop closed her door, she raised the privacy partition and collapsed in a fit of tears.

Chapter 7

Yolan looked through the tinted window as Troop pulled up to The Firm apartment parking garage. She was already dreading the long drive to Galveston with Monet cross examining her about Ryan, when she noticed Monet's convertible Mustang parked sideways blocking the entrance her hazards flashing, Shay was with her. Both were on their phones pacing.

Troop pulled up next to them and popped on his hazards, by the time he came around to open her door, Yolan was already rushing over to Monet and Shay tucking Angel into the back of her capri pants.

"What's up, where do I need to be?" Yolan asked, all self-pity and hurt she felt seconds ago shelved, her brain automatically shifted into lethal mode.

"The hospital. Sugar Bear ran Whisper's car off of the road about thirty minutes ago. Joy figures they are coming for you next, especially when they find out Bruise put a hot one in Sugar Bear's stupid ass, so she sent us to get you," Shay said while rushing towards her.

Yolan rushed to get into Monet's car, but Shay stopped

her. "No, ma'am, I drove one of The Firm's undercover bulletproofs over here, we're taking that." Shay pointed out the tricked out white Land Rover parked on the corner behind the parking garage.

"But how would they even know where I am? I haven't been to my house in months," Yolan asked, walking quickly with Shay to the Rover.

A split second later, she heard a body hit the ground. She turned around in alarm, worried about Monet only to see her standing over Troop, a bullet wound in his front temple.

Monet unscrewed her silencer as she rushed over to them and climbed into the driver's seat of the Rover.

"Jesus, Monet! What the fuck! Someone could have seen you and the security cameras? Oh my God, this day is an entire ass mess!" Yolan screamed from the back seat panicking, that move was dangerous and reckless.

She looked over her shoulder and watched the black cleaner van pull up and toss Troop inside, the blood stain on the sidewalk disappeared next, then the van.

Rini and Meika stepped up, each climbing behind the wheel of the two cars still flashing their hazards and calmly drove the town car and Monet's convertible away. It all went so fast it was almost like it never happened. Damn, The Firm was good!

Joy appeared next and walked over to them. "Why are you still here? You did your part. Now get to the hospital and stay with Whisper. Jazz has ordered a clean sweep, this 'Man' shit ends tonight."

Joy walked away still giving orders from her earpiece, just as they pulled around the corner and away from the building, they saw Joy's black on black Charger tear down a side street to handle business.

"Yolan, Troop was dirty, he was double crossing the crew, feeding intel to Man and Heavy's people. Me and Shay were just about to warn you when you pulled up. Oh, and why you worried about me being seen or the cameras? Did you forget who you worked with? The Firm shut the buildings down as soon as they heard about Whisper. Electricity off and phone towers scrambled, no way in or out. Besides, who are they going describe?" Monet asked and pulled up to a stop sign, Shay and Monet switched places 'Chinese fire drill style'.

Yolan watched Monet pull off the braided wig she thought was Monet's hair until two seconds ago and switch into a completely different outfit as they pulled up to the hospital, she pulled the bobby pins out of her own long hair. Meika walked past the car as they exited it and dropped Monet's keys in her hand and took the bag Monet had shoved the wig and clothes into. Not a word was spoken between them as it happened.

They spotted Jazz pacing back and forth on the maternity floor, as they rushed off the elevator.

He looked up and covered the distance between them swiftly.

"She's okay just a little banged up, she hit her head on the car door window, she's got some cuts and bruises from the broken glass. The baby's okay too, they are keeping her here a few nights for observation," he reported mechanically as soon as they were in ear shot.

That was the first time Yolan had ever seen Jazz not look like he walked off a men's fashion magazine.

"Thank God! If anything had happened to them, I would have taken Man apart piece by piece!" Monet said, looking hostile and hard.

Jazz shook his head looking down the hall to make sure no one was around them. "Get in line, that's one trigger I'm pulling myself but now that you said that I might take you along to have a little fun, Mo, cool?" Jazz offered walking them to Tayana's room.

"You know I'm down, Jazz. No one fucks with my family and especially not our Boss Lady, just say when and where and I'm there," Monet agreed, smiling her evil grin that always scared the hell out of Yolan.

"Jazz, please don't encourage her brand of crazy, at least not within earshot of all these people," Yolan said following him inside Tayana's room her heart still racing from the sudden turn of events that had just unfolded.

Tayana was laying in the bed, a bandage on her forehead, a few scratches on her right cheek. Monitors and machines beeped and rang as they monitored her and the baby's vital signs. As soon as her eyes met Yolan's, they both burst into tears.

Yolan rushed forward and threw her arms around Tayana. "I'm so sorry, Yo. I should have listened to you, I should have never let his ass go the first time he tried this shit!" Tayana sobbed loudly, her tears wetting Yolan's blouse.

***

"Wait, what the fuck did she just say, Yo?" Jazz demanded stepping closer to her and Tayana looking deadly.

Monet and Shay exchanged a look of confusion and surprise and sat down next to Tayana's bed silently.

Tayana sat up and looked over at Jazz, Monet, and Shay wiping her tears away. "I said I should have never let Man go when he pulled this shit the first time," she admitted softly, running her hands down her swollen belly.

"Baby, how hard did you hit your head? Because the Tayana I know would have never let him clear the doorway without a bullet in his temple," Jazz stated cautiously on the other side of her bed. Looking from her to Yolan for an answer.

"You want me to tell them, Tay or you? Either way it's past time they all knew." Yolan grabbed both of Tayana's hands and waited for her to answer.

Tayana sighed and sat back against her pillows shaking her head sadly.

"You can tell it, you remember more about it than I do," she said, taking Jazz's hand smiling tiredly.

Yolan got off the bed and closed the door to Tayana's room after telling the nurses they didn't want to disturb the other patients or be disturbed, they were going to perform a prayer circle.

She tuned the radio to a gospel station and turned it up loud, she then told everyone but Jazz to turn off their phones.

"As you two remember, there was a bit of a power struggle after Heavy died," Yolan said to Monet and Shay, as she sat back down on the other side of Tayana.

"Yeah, I remember Man thought he could coast on Heavy's name without putting in any work and tried to force us out because we were young and female. I remember we bought out Man's weak ass crew and he decided to go legit," Shay said quickly with a shrug looking over at Monet who agreed nodding.

"That's not entirely true. That's what I told you to protect Tay. Just like all we really said about Thirst was that he almost got Tayana killed but never said how. Instead of really leaving, Man went underground and had Thirst as the front man while he was giving the orders behind the scenes.

Man was pissed that not only did an all-female crew beat him, but an all-female crew run by his baby sister forced him out." Yolan paused and waited for everyone to catch on, Monet caught on first.

"Hold the fuck up. Thirst's dirty ass worked for Man!"

Monet asked loudly, looking like she wanted to dig him up and kill Thirst all over again.

"Shh but yes, Mo, Thirst worked for Man. I figured it out but not before Man almost got to Tay," Yolan admitted looking over at Tayana to make sure she was ready for her to tell the rest.

When she closed her eyes and nodded, laying her head on Jazz's chest, he had moved to the head of the bed and pulled her into his arms as Yolan was talking, she continued.

"Man wanted Tayana gang raped by his crew and then killed, you know as the ultimate humiliation for Tay and a message to the rest of us of what would happen if we continued to challenge him once Tayana was gone." Yolan paused to catch her breath, the memory of that day had her on the verge of vomiting.

"Thirst slipped her the date rape drug and she was fading fast. She knew something was wrong because as we all know Tay never drinks enough to even catch a buzz, she never has and texted me: '911, with Thirst'. When I got there, all six of those sick muthafuckas were in the living room, waiting for her to pass all the way out, arguing about who was going to go first and shit. Me and Joy dropped them like bowling pins, I told her to keep watch while I went to go get Tay and when I found her, Thirst was standing over her, she was out cold and he was bragging on the phone about how easy it was to woo her and asking if the person had any special requests before he violated her. I pressed my Angel to the back of his head and sent his ass to Hell with a quickness. He dropped his phone when he died and I was on a murder mission, whoever was on the other end of that fucking phone had a smoking hot bullet coming too, I picked the phone up and heard him shouting for Thirst, I grew up with that voice I knew who it was immediately."

Silent tears ran down Tayana's face as Yolan told them

what happened. Monet and Shay sat rigid and still in stunned silence looking from Yolan to Tayana in shock.

Yolan was watching the monitors, the room was filled with a thumping and swishing sound as the baby moved around, agitated.

Jazz put his hand on Tayana's stomach and kissed her on the forehead whispering something to her. The baby immediately began to calm down.

"It's okay, Yo, you can finish," Tayana said, taking the cup of water Monet poured and passed over to her.

"I know you guys remember Tay spending two days in the hospital and I was in and out never around much, well it was because I spent those two days on the hunt for Man. Everyone kept questioning why I kept disappearing. I gave vague answers and kept looking for him. I didn't care if when I found him he killed me too, just as long as he was riding the train to the afterlife with me." Yolan felt like fire ants were biting her all over as the anger she felt at that time awoke from its years long slumber.

"I had to make sure Tay and all of you guys were safe. Then just as I was closing in on him, he bitched up and messaged Tay, telling her to call off her dog. Of course, Tay had no fucking clue what he was talking about or that her brother, her full-blooded, raised in the same fucking house, same parents brother set her up to be gang raped and killed. She called me and told me to come where she was because she knew what I was doing but didn't understand why. Once I told her everything, she told me I couldn't kill Man because even though he was part Heavy, he was still part Essie and that part of him she still loved. She said if I ever loved her that was the time to prove it and stand down. I promised I wouldn't kill him but told her it was a mistake to let his snake ass live. Joy and Rini paid him a visit scaring him so bad he disappeared the next day." Yolan sighed and looked over at all four of them.

Jazz was still holding Tayana, rubbing her stomach lovingly but his eyes were dark and lethal. "Now his bitch ass is back and he has not only approached Yolan and threatened her, but he tried to kill his sister again. Only this time he fucked up royally because not only is she his sister, she also happens to be my wife and she's pregnant with my baby. Yeah, that junkie, mush brained, weak willed, punk's days are numbered," Jazz stated coldly pulling his phone out of his pocket as it vibrated.

Yolan moved across the room and turned down the radio just as Joy and Rini walked in, out of breath, looking stressed.

"Yo, I'm sorry. We fucked up, we were on our way there but we were still too slow to prevent it," Rini started to explain when at the same time Jazz surged to his feet in anger.

"What the fuck do you mean my cousin's place just got shot up!" he barked into the phone.

All the breath left Yolan's body and it felt like someone snatched her underwater. Her hearing was a bit muffled, and her eyesight was getting blurry, like a gauzy curtain had been pulled over her eyes.

Tayana sat up and gasped, looking over at Yolan her eyes wide. "Tay, you knew?" was the last thing Yolan said before she took two steps towards the door and passed out.

───────

Yolan's eyes felt like they had been doused in bleach as she struggled to open them, so she quickly closed them again. Stiff scratchy sheets dragged across her skin when she reached up to push her hair out of her face, the tug of something tethered to her wrist had her coming up short.

"Careful, you don't want to rip that thing out." Tayana's voice warned soft and quietly from the side of her bed.

Yolan forced her eyes open and turned towards her voice. Tayana was dressed in a soft silk ivory robe and matching gown, sitting in a wheelchair on the side of her hospital bed.

"What happened?" Yolan asked, her voice was raspy and she was trying to remember what happened. All her mind would tell her was Tayana had been hurt and it had something to do with Man. Something else majorly wrong, she should remember, played on the edge of her brain as well.

"You passed out and split the back of your head open, you have a concussion. They ran more tests too, those results aren't back yet. You've been unconscious for two days," Tayana answered just as quiet, her eyes filling with tears.

"Don't cry, Tay and what the hell are you doing out of bed? Are you and the baby okay?" Yolan asked with concern trying to sit up, her head started spinning and pounding at the same time, just as her stomach went sour, so she sat back closing her eyes again. She felt Tayana grab her hand and whisper, "Don't worry, we're fine, Yo," just as she passed out again.

"Does she know? Did you even have a chance to tell her that me and Ryan are related?"

Yolan was dreaming, in the dream she heard Jazz asking Tayana about him and Ryan. The light in the dream was soft and muted, the monitors in the room beeped in a steady rhythm.

"No, I didn't get a chance to tell her before all hell broke loose. I was going to tell her when we got to Galveston, but you already know that didn't happen," Tayana answered him with regret in her voice.

"Tayana, how long did you know? Why didn't you at least tell me about them seeing each other once you found out who he was to me?" Jazz asked, whispering and sounding a bit annoyed.

"Because as much as I love you, Jazz, Yolan needed to know first," Tayana explained firmly.

"You avoided my first question, Boss Lady, how long have you known that Ryan was my cousin?" Jazz insisted a little louder.

"A month, Joy told me a month ago. We didn't run a very thorough check on him at first because he was only a client, but when we saw how serious they were getting I had Joy run it and that's when I found out," Tayana admitted barely above a whisper.

"Then that's the day you should have told me and Yolan, Tayana," Jazz whispered back fiercely.

"Don't you think I know that now, Jazz? I'm so sorry I didn't tell either one of you as soon as I knew but I thought I was protecting her."

"Protecting her from who or what, Tayana?" Jazz whispered, sounding frustrated with his wife.

"Herself, Jazz, that's who! Because of who we grew up around and the line of work we dabble in, she has always sold herself short, convinced herself she's not worthy of love from someone like Ryan. Never mind the multi-million dollar real estate deals she's made, or the awards, or recognition Royalty continues to win. In her eyes, she feels like she will never be seen as good enough around people who are not a part of our world, especially men. Just because some asshole in her life told her she was nothing more than a ghetto girl and a hood rat and she believed him.

"She's put-up walls to protect herself from ever being hurt like that again. From the moment she met Ryan she has been freaked out about being with him, because she's convinced herself that all business types like Ryan are like her ex. So yes, I dragged my feet telling her, or even you, so my best friend and sister wouldn't sabotage her own happiness because I saw how much she liked him," Tayana whispered back emotionally.

"Do you think it's time for her to step down and work solely at Royalty? I know I'm still the new kid on the block, so to speak, but I love Yolan too and I want to see her happy. For the record though, Ryan would never hurt Yolan. Knowing my cousin and the way he is, I can tell he's in love with her, even if he won't admit it.

"He's pretty pissed at her right now, but she got his heart all the way open to her. Listen to me and hear me, Tayana, you have to promise me. We have to let them figure all this shit out on their own, and as for you, Boss Lady, no more secrets," Jazz stated on a sigh.

"Yes, Jazz, I promise. I'll stay out of it no matter how difficult that will be. As far as her stepping down, honestly that's on Yolan. If she wants to step down then she should, but I don't think she does, she loves working the crew and the reason why she is second in command is because she is good, damn good, at what she does.

"Even with my pregnancy causing me to take a step back, our crew is still the well-oiled machine it always has been because of Yolan, she just needs to know someone, somewhere will love her for her, period. None of that matters right now, though. I am going crazy! It's been three days since she talked to me. Why won't she wake back up? I just need her to be okay!" Tayana's voice broke as she sobbed.

"I know, Tayana, but remember the doctor said they discontinued the medication that was keeping her sedated this morning because the swelling in her brain has improved, so she should wake up soon but, in the meantime, you have to get some rest too. Pregnant or not I will still put some fire on that ass of yours. Now, Shay is on her way up to sit with Yolan and I'm taking you home to get some rest."

Those were the last words Yolan heard in her dream before tears escaped from beneath her closed eyelids and her dream faded to black.

Ryan watched two women moving swiftly down the hall on their cellphones as they walked out of her hospital room. He waited until they both stepped onto the elevator before silently, but quickly, stepping into the sterile, white room. He knew he didn't have much time before he would be noticed.

The machines inside the room beeped rhythmically, monitoring her vital signs as her soft breathing sounds caused him to sigh in relief. He closed the door and his heart pounded in his chest with concern, as he moved closer to her. She stopped him in his tracks, even with her head wrapped in bandages, oxygen in her nose and dark circles under her eyes she was still the most beautiful woman he had even seen. Despite their ugly exchange the last time they saw each other, his first impulse was to climb into the bed with her and hold her in his arms until she woke up, but right now, that wasn't an option.

Ryan had promised Jazz he would stay away from the hospital because of the risks to all of them but he had now broken that promise and was on borrowed time. He knew him being there was reckless as hell, but he had to come. The longer he sat in that damn apartment, not being able to see her, the crazier his imagination got. So before he completely lost his damn mind, he knew he had to come and check on her himself.

"Damn, Ny, you have no idea how worried I've been about you," Ryan said quietly as he reached down and lightly touched Yolan's sleeping face. "When Jazz came and told me what was going on, I just about lost my shit. Jazz had to physically restrain me because I didn't give a damn about what was going on, I just knew I was coming to see you," he told her with a soft chuckle shaking his head. "Honestly I have never come so close to fighting my cousin as I did that night." Ryan touched the soft section of hair that was peeking out of her bandages.

"You know, Ny, even with all of this shit going on, I will never understand why you felt you couldn't talk to me about this part of your life. But you better trust and believe that is going to change, because we will be talking about it and much more once you recover. So get used to seeing me because I'm not going anywhere," he said leaning down and kissing her softly on the lips, touching her soft skin again.

Ryan knew he sounded like a babbling idiot, he had so much he wanted to say but now was not the time to say it all, more than anything he just wanted her to know he was there. He found himself just standing next to the bed, staring down at her – thinking of the last time he'd heard her laugh – when he heard the clicking of high-heeled shoes on linoleum getting closer and knew he needed to leave.

He leaned down, kissing her again, before moving back towards the door to listen at it. When the hurried steps moved past Yolan's door, he cast one last look over his shoulder. "I love you, Ny, please hurry back to me," he whispered and slipped out of the room and back towards the stairwell closest to her room.

Ryan's over-protective mind was screaming. Telling him he couldn't leave her like this, for him to stay in the hospital until she was awake again. The ding of the elevator announced its arrival on the floor and echoed through the corridor. He saw two women, different from the ones he had seen when he first arrived, stepping off the elevator and starting to walk towards Yolan's room. He was able to relax a little bit knowing his cousin and his wife's team would protect her until he was able to again.

Yolan blinked blankly at the doctor as he went over the last of her test results before she was discharged. He breezed over them like what he just told her didn't change her life forever.

She was dressed and ready to leave, after twelve days in the hospital, five unconscious and seven conscious and cranky as ever, she was going the hell home and she couldn't wait. Now, right before she left, this damn doctor who she was sure began practicing in the late 1800's just knocked her off balance yet again! Holy Shit!

"Miss Belle, do you have any questions for me at this time?" the doctor asked her looking up from her chart and discharge summary.

Yolan stared at the tufts of fluffy white hair growing out of his ears, still in shock. Hell yeah she had questions, hundreds of them. But, first and foremost, her question was, *"Are you fucking kidding me!"* she thought to herself.

"No, I think you covered anything I would have asked," Yolan answered, pulling at a loose string on the blanket covering the bed, she was sitting in the chair next to it, ready to go as soon as Monet came to get her.

"Great, well here are your prescriptions and discharge papers and try not to overdo it, move back into your normal routine slowly. You still have a lot of healing to do, you hit your head pretty hard, so you're going to need to rest for the next few days. Also don't forget to schedule your follow up appointments, I would recommend making those when you get home and get settled," the elderly doctor said, smiling over at Yolan.

"Don't worry she will," Monet announced as she entered

the room smiling, flashing the doctor her thousand-watt smile before casting a no-nonsense glare at Yolan. "I will personally make sure she does," Monet promised and moved around the doctor hugging Yolan tight, when they pulled apart they were both quickly wiping away tears.

"Is there anything else she needs to do?" Monet asked, grabbing Yolan's bag and dropping it on her shoulder.

"As I said before, for the first few days she needs to take it easy. If there's no more questions, I will send in the nurse with the wheelchair so you can get out of here," the doctor said, looking from Yolan to Monet.

"No, and thank you, to you and your staff for taking such good care of me," Yolan said smiling over at the doctor still trying to wrap her head around everything he just told her.

"Yo, I swear to God if you ever do some shit like that again, I'm going to kill your ass!" Was the first thing Monet said as soon she had Yolan settled in the white Land Rover.

"Sure, Mo, I split the back of my head open on purpose causing a concussion and brain swelling just to annoy you, please forgive me for being so selfish," Yolan said sarcastically, glaring over at Monet with a smirk.

"I see that time in the hospital did nothing to curb that quick tongue and asshole gene of yours," Monet tossed back, smiling over at her batting her eyelashes playfully.

"You already know, that ain't ever going to change, but anyway what's going on with the clean sweep?" Yolan asked, turning in the passenger's seat to face Monet.

"Nope, Yolan don't even go there. Good God, Whisper knows your ass like the back of her hand! She told me to tell you if you asked about it, that business is being handled so relax and let the rest of us do the heavy lifting," Monet informed her looking over at her quickly then back at the road.

"Okay. But seriously I just need to know one thing—"

"He's fine, Yo. Jazz moved him himself. Jazz said he will tell you where he is when you're feeling better and up to it, now that's it, Yo," Monet said, cutting her off.

"Fine, Monet," Yolan said and sat back, closing her eyes because she felt a little car sick.

───────

"Yolan, wake up, Boo, we're here," Monet whispered, tapping Yolan on the shoulder gently.

Yolan opened her eyes slowly and looked out the car window, they were parked in front of a house she had never seen before.

"Where are we, Mo?" she asked stretching her arms over her head, she had no intention of falling asleep but obviously her body had other plans.

"We're in Plano. We had to move everyone who could work remotely out here until the sweep is finished so here we are, welcome home," Monet explained, taking the keys out of the car.

Yolan slowly got out of the car and looked around. The house was one of seven in the same area, a huge plantation style house with wrap around porches and was in the center of the cul-de- sac like compound.

They were surrounded by trees and off to the right was a small lake and sitting area.

"Who's all here?" Yolan asked looking around still, it was so quiet she could hear the crickets and cicadas chirping.

"So far, it's just you, Neutral, Butchie and Whisper. Jazz drives down every other day and, of course, we have security here in both houses on the ends. There is a privacy fence with a code to enter the property as well. Jazz's main concern was keeping everyone safe and out of the line of fire, especially you guys since you seem to be Man's primary targets," Monet informed her walking up to the house in front of them.

"Asia too, huh? Did Man and them come for her and Butchie too?" Yolan asked, concerned. She stepped into the house and looked around in amazement, it was beautiful and furnished remarkably close to the style of her house in Houston.

She wandered to the kitchen and smiled at the small garden right outside the kitchen in the sunroom.

"No, but considering how they came for Ryan, when they couldn't get to you, we figured Asia would be next so we got ahead of them. Whisper picked and decorated this house for you herself, drove everyone crazy trying to make sure it was done in time," Monet informed her looking up at the vaulted ceilings.

"Do you like it, Yo?" Tayana asked cautiously, walking down the three steps from the entryway to the living room. Her belly was slightly bigger than the last time Yolan saw her, she actually waddled a bit now.

Yolan was looking over her shoulder at Tayana scanning her for injuries from her car accident, she silently thanked God that she only had a faint scar on her forehead now, she was relieved to see she had healed so well.

She hated to admit that it kind of hurt to see Tayana, knowing now, that she knew about Ryan being related to Jazz and didn't tell her. "It's beautiful, I mean if you have to lay low this is most definitely the way to do it. Thanks, Tay," Yolan answered and looked back out at the garden.

"Mo, Shay just got here about fifteen minutes ago, she said there are some things you guys need to wrap up with Diamond before you guys close for the remodel," Tayana informed Monet, moving further into the living room.

Monet's eyes grew in alarm as she looked down at herself, she was wearing jeans and a nice blouse, sandals with her hair in a French twist, light colored lipstick stained her lips.

"Well shit! Is Diamond with her?" Monet asked, panicking.

To Yolan she looked as beautiful as always, but knowing Monet, she felt she looked a mess because she wasn't runway fierce.

"Girl, no. Diamond ain't here now, calm down, damn! She's in the main house," Tayana scolded and sat down on the couch shaking her head as she watched Monet leave. "I swear that girl gets so crazy when you mention that man's name," Tayana said, shaking her head.

Yolan moved back into the living room and sat down across from Tayana, laughing a little. "Yeah, she does, she's got it bad too," Yolan said, slipping off her shoes, loving how the plush carpeting felt between her toes. "I'm glad to see you and the little one are doing okay," she stated, looking over at Tayana again.

"Yep, getting stronger every day. What about you, what all did the doctor say?" Tayana asked standing back up and moving over to the couch Yolan was sitting on.

"He said I suffered a concussion, that I was in a drug induced coma for three days because of the brain swelling but there's no damage or anything from that, thank God. I'm okay but I still feel off, he said that should go away in time and of course I have follow up care to schedule. My stitches itch like hell but I guess that means I'm healing," Yolan answered evenly looking down at her hands.

"Do you hate me, Yolan?" Tayana asked nervously, her eyes filling with tears.

Yolan shrugged and kept her eyes on her hands. "I could never hate you, Tay, you know that. You have to understand I knew that you knew for all of about thirty seconds before I passed out. I did have a dream when I was in the hospital about you though, I dreamed you and Jazz were talking about how you knew about him and Ryan and why you waited to tell me, in my dream your answer made me cry." Yolan looked over at Tayana, tears gathering in her eyes as she spoke.

Tayana frowned and shook her head slowly. "That wasn't a dream, Yo. Me and Jazz were sitting next to your bed talking. I was hoping you'd wake up so we could at least talk a little bit before Jazz sent me out here to Plano."

"Wow, this pregnancy really has made you soft, normally you would have told Jazz to go straight to hell for trying to take you to the country," Yolan chuckled, shaking her head and sitting back against the couch.

"True, the old me would have but with everything that's happened, my wants are not the only wants that matter. Anyway, I didn't want to keep things from you, I thought I was doing this for your own good, I pray to God you know that," Tayana said, placing her hands on Yolan's squeezing lightly.

"I get it, Tay. But I would be lying if I said I wasn't pissed off at you for a hot minute," Yolan admitted, squeezing Tayana's hand back.

"As you should be, but please do me a favor? Can you not pay me back by scaring the hell out of me next time? Yolan there was so much blood! I was literally standing in the middle of my bed screaming at the top of my lungs, I thought you got shot at first! I ripped my IV out trying to get to you. It was a mess." Tayana shivered remembering the chaos from that day she showed Yolan the scar on the back of her hand where she ripped out her IV.

"Trust me, it wasn't on purpose! I got up to leave the room and call Ryan. I knew he probably hated me, but I just needed to know he was okay and then the next thing I knew I was in a hospital bed."

"Just so you know, Yo, he's okay. Jazz checks in with him

every day. He claims he's done trying to be with you but then asks about you in the next breath, he's been driving Jazz crazy," Tayana informed her, smiling over at her softly.

"He will stop asking about me once all of this craziness dies down, then he can work on hating me for real." Yolan sighed, fighting back the onslaught of hopeless tears.

"Oh, please stop, little miss drama queen," Tayana quipped, rolling her eyes at Yolan and shaking her head. "It won't matter if he really does or doesn't hate you anyway. I mean you two have to talk and soon right?" Tayana asked looking over at Yolan with a knowing smile.

"Of course you know, you really are unbelievable, Tay. Does anything ever get past you?" Yolan asked folding her arms and sitting back on the couch. Her head was starting to hurt. "Just do me a solid, Tay and please keep things under wraps for now, I will cross that bridge when I'm ready to cross it. Right now, my life is all too fucked up and I need to get back on track before I can even begin to have that deep of a talk with Ryan," Yolan stated, shaking her head over at Tayana.

"Ugh you are so damn annoyingly stubborn and you know I won't say anything, not even to Jazz, but not telling Ryan right away is not fair, Yolan. You know that, right?" Tayana asked shaking her head again moving to sit next to Yolan on the couch. "Nevertheless, I missed you so much, Yo. I was going crazy without our morning phone calls!" Tayana exclaimed, throwing her arms around Yolan's neck and pulling her in for a hug.

"I missed you, too, Tay, but you have got to stop with all this emotional shit. You're killing me," Yolan said hugging her back, tears falling down her face.

"Yeah, it is a bit out of control ain't it? This baby is going to be evil as hell with all the tears I've been crying. Anyway, if you feel up to it, once you get settled you should come up to the main house and have dinner. Jazz is coming up tonight and he can bring you up to speed on everything going on with the clean sweep."

"Girl, yes. Just let me get showered and I will be on my way. What is Ms. Lanie cooking?" Yolan asked with renewed energy and excitement, wiping tears away.

"Fried chicken, butter beans, and the trimmings," Tayana informed her and called her after walking over to the front door, "And Yo?"

"Yeah Tay? And I swear to God if you make me cry again, I'm kicking your ass as soon as that baby drops!" Yolan warned Tayana looking over at her.

"Welcome to the club," Tayana teased and closed the door behind her.

Chapter 8

Yolan walked into the main house carrying some green onions for Ms. Lanie from her garden, Tayana was craving fried green onions and eggs and was driving them all bat shit crazy, especially since the green onions in the fridge at the main house had gone bad.

Clean sweep was still in full effect and she had tried to reach out to Ryan but he sent her call to voicemail and sent a simple text stating he was glad she was okay but was not in the frame of mind to talk to her yet ,she cried for two days but took the hint that he was done with her and tried to focus on the tasks at hand. Every day she woke up from dreams of him with a smile on her face only to be disappointed when she realized he wasn't actually there. Needless to say she cried a lot more than she laughed most days.

"Thank you, Yolan. Chile, I thought I was going to have to tie her down the way she was carrying on this morning! Now what can I make for you?" Ms. Lanie asked, smiling lovingly over at Yolan.

They had been up in Plano for two months, her headaches

were gone, and she worked four hours a day remotely with Asia to keep Royalty on top.

All of Heavy's old team including Sugar Bear and their younger associates were no longer amongst the living but Man was still slinking around causing trouble. He attempted to break into Tayana's gallery and the salon with no success, but by the time The Firm got there he had disappeared again. They all concluded he had some other crew working with him too but so far, they had remained invisible.

She had made and went to all of her follow up appointments and was told she was headed in the right direction health wise. She hated pills but managed to choke down the ones she was prescribed daily.

"Honestly, Ms. Lanie, I don't usually have an appetite this early in the morning nowadays so I'm good, but thank you for looking out for me," Yolan answered as she brewed herself a cup of ginger tea for her upset stomach and picked up a few crackers Ms. Lanie seemed to have started setting out just for her.

"Uh huh, you still need to keep your strength up, you're still healing. I'm scrambling you an egg and making you some dry toast," Ms. Lanie announced taking the crackers out of Yolan's hand and shooing her out of the kitchen.

She ran into Jazz on her way out. "Hey, I thought you weren't coming until tomorrow." Yolan saw the serious look on his face and pointed to the back of the house. "She's on the sun porch," Yolan informed him and quickly followed him when he motioned to her that she should.

"Baby, hi, I thought you weren't coming up until– what's up?" Tayana stopped smiling and asked, sitting up in alarm.

"The house in Galveston was broken into early this morning. This sneaky bastard is pissing me the fuck off and when I find out who's feeding him information and helping his ass,

I'm wrecking their shit too!" Jazz snapped and sat down next to Tayana; his hands clenched in fists.

"How is it that this junkie, bitch made bastard is getting all this fucking help? I mean who the fuck are these people? No one we work with would even lower themselves to work with Man so it has to be somebody desperate, somebody from the outside who doesn't have shit to lose," Yolan said thoughtfully sitting across from them getting upset.

She was tired of this shit! She hadn't seen the inside of her own house in months, and here she thought Whisper was going to lose it in the country, but she was the one about to snap. She wanted to drive back to Houston to find Man her damn self and end this shit once and for all.

"Yolan, I know that look and you ain't going. You, of all people, can't go back to Houston right now, it's almost like he's gunning for you even more than he's gunning for me, and he knows him hurting you would be the best way to hurt me. I love all my lethal ladies, but he knows you and me are even tighter," Tayana reminded her with a stern look and a raised eyebrow.

"Yeah, don't you think I know that, Tay? I just want my life to go back to normal. I want to take my Angel and let her sing until she loses her fucking voice on these pieces of shit fucking with my goddamn family!" Yolan broke down covering her face as she sobbed in frustration.

"Yo, you have to calm down or you're going to make yourself sick. I know how you feel because I feel the same way, but we have to play it smart, and you know that. I know this life frustrates you sometimes, it can be frustrating to me too and sometimes to maintain what we have and keep our operations moving smoothly we have to make sacrifices. We are in the middle of a war and war ain't never pretty," Tayana told Yolan, her own eyes welling up with tears.

"You know what, Tay? That reminds me of a question

Jazz asked you about me wanting to step down, the answer is and will always be *hell no*. This is my life, this is my family and whoever I end up with, will learn to fuck with that or not, I ain't going nowhere!" Yolan snapped and stood because Ms. Lanie was ringing her bell announcing breakfast was ready.

"Is Ryan this damn bad?" Tayana asked, shaking her head watching Yolan's retreating back.

"Boss Lady, believe it or not he's even worse," Jazz told her, helping her up so they could go eat breakfast.

"By our count the last one standing is Man but obviously he got another crew working for him we just need to find out who the fuck they are and take care of their asses too," Joy stated from her end of the dining room table.

Tayana called for all her ladies on deck in Plano, after Jazz's news, two days later on Thursday morning. Asia aka Neutral was even at the table for this one.

"True enough, Joy but I called you all here to make sure we are all on the same page. Until that little maggot is found and dealt with we are all in holding patterns, our businesses are running with security staff, skeleton crews, or not at all and we cannot continue like this indefinitely. So I wanted to ask you all what we should do moving forward? Instead of me calling the shots for all of us because you have all made your businesses the successes they are, not me, and you know what your clientele needs," Tayana stated looking around at all of them, taking a pause to take a bite of the cubed yellow-meat watermelon next to her.

"Yolan and Neutral, Royalty is one of the businesses that is still moving but the brick-and-mortar building has not been in use in over two months, so I'm asking you two first, do you ladies want to return to Houston and open back up or continue to work remotely from here? We can increase security if need be to keep you and your staff safe." Tayana looked over at them both and waited for their answer.

Asia cleared her throat and looked around at all of them, the badass women she grew up with and sighed, "I'm all about our clients and doing what makes them happy and making money moves, but anyone who is crazy enough to orchestrate the sick shit Man did *before* he was on drugs cannot not be slept on, something is wrong with that fool and until either Jazz or Joy say he's no more I'm cool staying here and working remotely. But if Yolan wants to head back, she's not going alone." Asia looked over at Yolan and waited for her to speak.

"It's a hard call but we are still addressing our clients' needs, so I'm with you Asia, we stay here until this is done. I hate being away from home, but I could never live with myself if something happened to one of our people because of Man." Yolan smiled over at Asia and looked up the table at Tayana who was scribbling down notes.

One by one the entire crew voted to stay the course for the safety of everyone and keep the businesses operating as they were.

"I had a suggestion I wanted to run past you, since we are all here for the weekend or at least until late Saturday night going into Sunday morning," Yolan stated looking at Joy, Rini and Meika who were going to head back to continue handling business in Houston late Saturday night. "I was thinking we could have the baby shower here instead of the beach house. It is a safer and more controlled environment and even Jazz and Butchie will be here. Instead of having everything delivered we can just pick everything up we're going to need. What do you guys think?" Yolan asked, making a mental note to reach out to the furniture store about the bassinets.

"Good idea, Yo. We have two of the bullet proofs up here so we can roll out in the morning to grab everything," Shay said, nodding, pulling out a blank piece of paper to start a list, her pen was scratching across the paper at lightning speed.

"Yeah, but baby showers are for females, Jazz and Butchie will be bored to tears," Asia said doubtfully, making a face.

"I thought of them too, game night with wings at your house, Asia. I called around and we can order the wings as late as tomorrow at noon, at two different places, for Saturday pickup, so we just need to know how many to order for them. Can The Firm spare a couple of Jazz's boys to be here too?" Yolan said.

"Well ladies?" Tayana asked around the table, already in better spirits.

"I say let's do this! We need some laughter and love in this camp!" Jaidyn said getting up from the table. "But on a kind of more important note is Ms. Lanie around? I am dying for a hot damn, got damn sandwich for lunch," Jaidyn said rubbing her hands together.

Asia looked around at everyone who was verbally agreeing with Jaidyn excitedly like they were crazy. "Um hold up, can someone please tell me what a hot damn, got damn sandwich is?" Asia asked with her hands upturned in question.

"It's a grilled ham and cheese sandwich with an over easy egg and fresh spinach on sourdough. It is a religious experience the way Ms. Lanie makes it, I promise you! I think Ms. Lanie puts crack in them or something! And what kind of friends are you, Yo and Whisper? This poor pregnant chile has been here this long and never had one?" Jaidyn asked, pressing her hand to her chest in horror, shaking her head.

Tayana looked from Jaidyn to Yolan, fighting back a smile. "The worst kind, I guess, Jaidyn. I haven't had one of those in months! You in Neu?" she asked Asia, finishing up her watermelon, her face lit up with excitement.

"Shit, the way everyone is in here drooling like savages, I'd be a fool not to be," Asia said looking around at all of them, a look of confusion on her face as Rini and Monet sat next to each other chanting, *Hot damn Got damn* while dancing in their seats.

"Meeting adjourned, our stomachs have spoken," Tayana laughed and stood up with some difficulty and led the line to the kitchen and Ms. Lanie.

Yolan stayed behind and grabbed the trash can nearest to her and threw up, the thought of her once favorite Ms. Lanie sandwich had her stomach turning inside out. "This shit is for the birds," she mumbled, grabbing her empty cup to go make herself another cup of ginger tea.

"I'm just saying how come all the fellas get is wings, though?" Jazz said loudly and laughing, watching as Ms. Lanie started putting platters on the dining room table.

"Because the preggos are at our party and this is what they asked for," Yolan answered back, laughing at him, Butchie, Bruise, Pain and Goon as they eyeballed the spread for the baby shower.

"Now I asked you guys to help hang the streamers and balloons that's it, or if y'all are staying to eat y'all are also playing party games with us, oohing and ahhing at all the gifts with no complaints *plus* you have to bring the wings back over here to share your food too!" Yolan threatened, glaring at all of them, her hands on her hips and still laughing.

The men all looked at each other then looked at the spread of mini lobster rolls, crab cakes, crab claws, two-bite mini quiches, fresh fruit, petit fours, Ms. Lanie's egg pie and a multilayered cake.

"All right bet!" they all said in unison, rubbing their hands together in preparation to eat.

Yolan moved in between them and the table. "Oh hell no,

I meant you could eat later *after* we finish decorating and at the shower, you damn savages!" she scolded, handing them each something to blow up or hang for the shower.

An hour later the shower was in full swing, everyone was laughing and talking, old school music played in the background.

Yolan was bent over with laughter as she watched Butchie and Jazz trying to tie their shoes with a balloon under their shirts. The tears streaming down her face were suddenly dried as someone opened the back door that led into the kitchen, letting in a warm autumn breeze.

Yolan looked over her shoulder assuming it was Bruise coming back with more ice for the drinks the guys were consuming, the ladies were all drinking sherbet punch. Her mouth dropped open in surprise and horror as his eyes met hers.

Chapter 9

"Sorry I'm late, Cuzzo, traffic was a bitch," Ryan said to Jazz, but his eyes were glued to Yolan's planting her in place, as he moved into the great room. Once he got close enough for her to smell his cologne, he shifted his gaze to Jazz.

"It's all good, you're here now, glad you got my text about the change of plans," Jazz said, waddling up to Ryan dabbing him up smiling.

"Umm, what the fuck did I walk in on?" Ryan asked, laughing at Jazz's balloon belly as he pushed the balloon up higher and pulled his silk, short-sleeved button down over it to keep it from escaping.

"Well, your cousin and Butchie here are constantly teasing me and Neutral about how long it takes us to do anything so we challenged them to do some of the normal things we have to do, like tie their shoes with a belly. I'm Whisper, by the way, or you might have heard me referred to as Tay, short for Tayana, or the annoying nickname your cousin gave me Boss Lady," Tayana explained, walking up to him smiling, extending her hand.

Ryan's face spread in a warm welcoming smile as he grabbed Tayana into a hug. "Girl, we're family, we don't shake hands, we hug! It's nice to finally meet you! Damn, Jazz, your descriptions of her were weak! This woman is fine!" He smiled, looking down at Tayana when he let her go, nodding his head in approval.

"Yeah, I already know, that's why I married her. So you and them light brown eyes, all the girls used to swoon over, need to fall all the way back," Jazz teased pulling Tayana close to his side.

"Whatever Jazz, you already know where my heart is but anyway, Ryan are you hungry? There's plenty of food in the dining room, beers in the fridge too." Tayana pointed everything out to him and walked back over to Yolan who was holding up the wall watching them all interact in silence.

"Girl! Why are you standing here like a fucking statue? Go talk to him!" Tayana hissed, shoving her lightly towards the dining room and Ryan's direction.

"Tay, I love you but that might change in the next ten seconds, please tell me you did not invite him here," Yolan said, turning back around to face Tayana, she was shaking from head to toe. Her hormones and emotions were all over the place. Why did he have to be so damn fine? More than that, why had their time apart only made her love for him grow even more? Those eyes Jazz had referred to definitely had her swooning!

"No, I didn't invite him, Yo. Jazz did, he wanted me to finally meet him before his godchild is born," Tayana said, smiling slyly and running her hand down her pregnant belly.

"Godchild? Really, Tay! Need I remind you this man is the reason I cried my eyes out for weeks when I first got here? I swear to God I don't know who to strangle first, you or Jazz, ugh, y'all make me sick!" Yolan whispered fiercely and turned to go start bringing Tay and Asia's gifts into the great room.

She walked right into Ryan who was smiling that fucking sexy smile of his chewing on a lobster roll.

"Careful, Yolan, don't want you to hurt yourself." He took another bite of his food as his eyes took a leisurely stroll up and down her body.

Yolan missed that look so much her thighs automatically went up in flames, fucking hormones! "Sorry about that, Ryan. I need to go get the gifts from the other room before it gets too late, some of our friends are driving back to Houston tonight," Yolan explained, quickly walking away backwards still facing him, before turning and rushing to the other room.

"Here let me help you, it looks like the 'daddies to be' are still struggling with their shoes," Ryan offered, setting his plate down on the end table to his right, shaking his head at Jazz and Butchie and chuckling before falling into step behind her.

"Shitfire and Fuck!" Yolan swore under her breath before she forced herself to smile. "Thanks, I appreciate it," she said over her shoulder and led him to the office full of shower gifts.

"Damn! Did y'all rob a baby store or something? You do realize they are having one baby each, right?" Ryan asked looking at all the gifts piled inside the room in amazement.

"Yes, Ryan we are aware of that fact. But because these are the first babies of the crew, they are coming into the world in style if we have anything to say about it," Yolan explained while moving the smaller boxes around looking for the bassinets. Her plan was to pile the smaller gifts inside of those and roll them out into the great room.

"I'll keep that in mind," Ryan said quietly, suddenly deep in thought watching her move.

"What?" she asked as she caught him staring.

"Nothing. Just been so long since I saw you, I was just making sure my dreams and memories were doing you justice," he quipped, his voice low and sexy. He leaned on the door frame, still staring her up and down as she moved around the desk.

"Whatever Ryan, you can save all of that charm and charisma for the next female, besides I thought you came in here to help me with the gifts, not hold up the wall," Yolan said, tossing him a scathing look over her shoulder, annoyed that he even had the nerve to say something like that to her especially after rejecting her. The fact the bassinets weren't where they should be was pissing her off too.

"I see some things never change huh, Yolan? I mean I know it's been a while but you know how I get down. That wall of insecurity is still strong as ever." He sneered giving her a hard, deadpan look. "What are you looking for anyway? I'm so much taller than you I might have a better vantage point over this sea of gifts than you do," he stated, looking annoyed.

"Two bassinets, one with ivory lace and one with white lace," she answered, trying her best not to notice, that even irritated and not smiling, he still looked damn near edible to her. All she wanted to do was move into his space and have him take her into his arms and carry her off somewhere like he used to. But she needed to shelf those feelings once and for all and focus on more important things when it came to the two of them.

"I don't see them, could you have put them somewhere else by mistake? I can go look around," he offered.

"No, that's okay, we wrapped all the gifts at my house this afternoon. I guess Bruise and Pain forgot to bring them over with everything else, I will just go get them. Do me a favor and start moving these to the table with all the balloons and stuff? I'll sort them out when I get back," Yolan asked, and moved to walk past him out of the office. He caught her lightly by the arm.

"After this is all over, we need to talk, Yolan," Ryan stated with a serious look on his face.

"Yeah we do need to talk, Ryan but here is not the time or place for it and it's not about us either. The way I see it, though, we tried it, it didn't work out and there is no reason to continue to torture each other until whatever was between us is replaced with animosity and hate," Yolan said and moved out of his grasp and started walking towards the back door to take the path that led to her house.

He caught up with her in two long strides, blocking her path. "Do you think I'm stupid or something, Yo? That I can't see what's up? Like I said, after the party you and me need to talk." Ryan's face was set in a hard stare, she had never seen him look at her like that before.

"Fine, Ryan, let's not do this here, and since when do you call me Yo?" she asked with a frown, not liking at all how her nickname sounded when he said it.

"Did it sound like I was asking or something? And I called you Yo because, right now? Knowing what I know, and you not saying a word about it, is something someone other than Yolan, and especially Ny, would ever do no matter what was going on between us." He continued to look at her with that hard stare.

"Whatever, Ryan," Yolan snapped, and stormed out of the back door, seething mad and hurt at the same time. Who was he to tell her how Yolan or Ny or even Yo would do any goddamn thing? Yeah, they would talk but on her fucking terms not his!

She let herself into the back door of her place and rushed over to the corner where both the bassinets were and noticed the guys forgot a few other gifts too and quickly tossed the small boxes inside one of the bassinets. She tried to use one hand on each to push them out and over to the main house but the wheels kept turning making them veer off course so it was clear she would have to take them over one at a time.

"Just great! How in the hell did they miss the damn things

anyway?" she snapped, pulling out her phone to call Monet to come help her.

"What's up, Yo? Long time no see," A familiar male voice said calmly, stepping up behind her.

She chuckled as she dropped her head forward remembering her own words, *Whoever hooked up with Man would be a desperate ass crew from the outside with nothing to lose.* She should have fucking known!

"What's up, Blue?" Yolan said turning around slowly, Angel rested in the holster on her ankle, because of the cut of her blouse, so her gun was out of reach, fuck!

"Man said if I kept an eye on your boy, he would lead me straight to you bitches, he's one smart motherfucker ain't he, Yo?" Blue stated, nodding, walking up on her slowly his gun pointed at her.

"No, you're both dumb as fuck, Blue, there is security all over this place, so even if you kill me, you won't make it out of here alive." Yolan smiled at him venomously as he moved closer.

"At this point why the fuck would I care! As long as your bitch ass is no longer breathing then my mission is complete. You see Whisper is more of a long-term goal for Man, the first thing he wanted was to get her 'ankle biting bitch' out of the way. His words, not mine, so here we are."

Blue extended his arm and pressed the gun to her forehead, since he was so close Yolan could see he was more nervous than he was trying to appear. His brows were covered in sweat, his eyes moved from her to scan the room several times, which made him more dangerous than someone in control, the only thing working in her favor was he was the type that getting in his head would be easy.

"Okay then, Blue, bring the pain, pull the trigger, see you on the other side," Yolan said tightly, her eyes boring into his, not blinking or with a drop of fear.

His face registered surprise that she wasn't afraid, wasn't begging for her life, she was as calm as she was the day her and the ladies held the power in their hands. His hand shook and his finger slipped off the trigger which made her relax even more. He shifted his weight from one foot to the other as he looked at her, biting his bottom lip nervously, his hesitancy exposing how weak he really was.

Seconds ticked by, the gun still pressed against her head. She thought of several ways she could attempt to disarm him but most would still have her ending up with a bullet wound so that was a no go.

He pulled out his phone with his other hand and unlocked it. "I'm going to call Man, have him come up here and take all you bitches down tonight!" he said smiling again, looking inspired, liking his new plan.

With the gun still at her forehead and his thumb poised over the number 2, who she assumed was Man on speed dial, a shot rang out and whizzed past her head and into Blue's shoulder forcing him backwards and the gun from her forehead.

Yolan dropped to the ground as Blue pulled the trigger instinctively, the gun was too big for him, and the recoil knocked him on his ass. Yolan moved in and brought her knee down on his wrist, breaking it before he could fire the gun again, it clattered against the wall after she slid it away from his reach with her foot.

"I fucking hate you, bitch! How the fuck a girl crew gonna shut us down and run us out of town!" Blue spat at Yolan, grimacing in pain, blood flowed from his shoulder like a faucet onto the tan carpet in her living room.

Yolan looked down at him and saw him for what he really was, he was a little kid with a bruised ego playing a grown person's game. He should have taken the chance he was given and kept it moving, but sadly, now he was going to see what his ego and listening to Man were going to cost him.

"Because you're a little bitch, lady crew or not, our balls are bigger than yours will ever be You weren't even man enough to pull the trigger, you pussy! " Yolan snapped and brought her elbow down on his face breaking his nose.

She was beyond pissed the fuck off! After everything she had been through in the past two months this idiot had the nerve to show up in her house, press a gun to her head, *and* bleed all over her carpet, after they gave them a chance to live after what Freeze pulled? Stupid little coward, she should have eliminated his ass with Freeze!

She finally looked up and over to see who shot Blue, and blinked in surprise when Ryan walked into the living room re-holstering his gun, looking lethal. What in the entire fuck!

"Damn Yo, Jazz warned me you are dangerous with or without a weapon. I see what he meant, your ass is scary!" he said, standing over Blue, shaking his head and admiring Yolan's handy work, while looking down at Blue's bloody face.

"Um... pardon the fuck. Care to explain to me why you not only have a gun, but you're like a fucking marksman or some shit, like slowly?" Yolan asked feeling herself getting lightheaded from the shock of the situation. "Holy shit! Did you know you could hit him without hitting me or did you just take a chance?" Yolan glared up at him as she messaged Joy to send someone to take out some 'trash'.

"Of course, I knew I could take the shot, Yolan. And wow, Jazz was right, you really have no idea, I thought he was full of shit." Ryan marveled looking over at her in annoyed amusement.

"What Ryan? What do I have no idea about now? You and Jazz, are you more than cousins? Long lost brothers maybe?" Yolan snapped throwing major attitude at Ryan still trying to wrap her head around what happened. "Who the hell are you? Are you a fucking secret agent? What am I clue-less about now? I swear to God, you, Jazz and Tay and all these fucking secrets are working my last fucking nerve!" she exclaimed, her voice echoed around the room as she stood glaring up at him, trying her hardest not to get riled up and emotional.

"Yo, I'm Jazz's second in command. Everything you are to Whisper I am to Jazz. Like I said when he told me about how precise and thorough The Firm was, I was sure they exposed me and you knew, but you just didn't tell Jazz you did," he said casually, turning around and chucking his chin at Pain and Goon as they rushed in.

"So, I saw his boys at the houses on either side of this one too, I took care of them both before I came here. No sign of that fucking cluck head, Man though, he sent little kids to do his dirty work. Guess he has no one else to hide behind now, fucking coward," Ryan said and moved closer to Yolan as they snatched Blue to his feet.

"Damn Reaper did you have to fuck him up this bad? Shit! He's making a fucking mess!" Goon complained, beginning to drag Blue out the room, trying not to get covered in his blood.

"Now you know that's not my style, the bullet wound? All me, but the rest? That was all Yolan here, guess he really pissed her off," Ryan said, shrugged and looked down at Yolan who was still looking up at him like he was a fucking stranger.

Did Goon just call Ryan 'Reaper'? No other words were spoken as they took Blue out the front door of the house and left them alone.

"Once the cleaner gets here, I'll make sure we get that carpet taken care of too. Now, shall we take these bassinets over and enjoy the rest of the party?" Ryan asked moving over to push one of them, he looked over his shoulder for her when she didn't move next to him to move the other one.

Yolan was still standing in the same place in stunned

silence. He was Jazz's second in command? Again, what in the actual entire fuck!

"Yo, like I said before you stomped off over here, we have a lot to discuss and we will talk later but until then shake it off, cool?" Ryan asked looking over at her, his normal warm gaze was in place again.

"Cool? No, Ryan or Reaper or whatever the fuck your name is, it's not cool! You just laid some seriously heavy shit at my feet and clapping it up while Tay and Asia open their gifts is not going to distract me from it! How could you not tell me about how deeply involved you were in Jazz's operation? And stop calling me Yo, I don't like it!" she demanded beginning to pace back and forth,

She had agonized over him not understanding her line of work and here he is second in command to Jazz! To Jazz! Their operations merged after he and Tayana got married but they had never met his second because, according to Jazz, he liked to stay undercover.

Never in a million years could she have ever imagined it was strait-laced, by the book, 'I want things the way I want them, when I want them', Ryan Fucking Devoe!

"Oh, you mean like you did about you and Whisper? Oh, that's right, you didn't! Besides that, you never gave me a fucking chance to! I didn't even know who the fuck you really were until Jazz picked me up after my place got shot up and told me! Even after seeing that shit with Man and your gun I still never connected the dots. And you're one to talk about someone not telling you something when you haven't even told me you're pregnant... Yo!" Ryan snapped, walking back over to where she was, he used her nickname she hated as a dig again.

Yolan stopped pacing and it felt like all the air had been sucked from the room as she looked up at him once again in shock and awe.

"How did you– Shit, never mind, Jazz must have told you," Yolan said quietly, sitting down on the couch shaking her head. She knew Tayana knew but she had sworn she wouldn't tell anyone, she must have let it 'slip' to Jazz.

"No, my cousin didn't tell me, but if he knew and didn't let me know? I got some choice words for his ass too," Ryan snapped, standing in front of Yolan with his arms folded, looking serious again.

"Then how? I know Tay wouldn't have told you, especially since she doesn't really know you," Yolan reasoned looking up at him with a frown.

"No one had to tell me, Yolan," he said, shrugging and shaking his head, his irritation softening a little.

"I have examined every inch of your body since I met you, with and without clothes, run those memories of you and of us over and over again in my head on a constant loop at night over the last two months. All it took was one look to notice your breasts are bigger, your hips are slightly wider and then there is the little bulge in your stomach where there was no bulge before. Maybe later you can explain to me why you didn't tell me yourself." Ryan sat next to her and placed his huge arm across her lower abdomen. "It's my baby too, you know," Ryan stated just as the doorbell rang.

"That will be the cleaners, let's get these other things over to the house and we can pick up this conversation later," Ryan suggested and helped her to her feet, she walked over and let them in and started to push one of the bassinets towards the back door, he followed behind her.

"Hmm, looks like something else got a little bigger too," he remarked, she looked over her shoulder and just like she thought his eyes were glued to her ass.

"So, are we talking here or at your house?" Ryan asked leaning on the counter in the kitchen as she loaded the dishwasher.

Despite the distraction of Blue and his boys, the shower had been an amazing success. Asia and Tayana could have their babies tomorrow and be set with diapers, wipes, bottles, and clothes to last them for at least two months.

"My house, just let me finish up here and we can walk over," Yolan said looking over her shoulder. Her head was still spinning with all he told her before they came back over to the party.

"Cool, I'll help. Where did Jazz and Whisper go?" he asked, looking around the now quiet house. Monet and Shay had gathered up all the trash and wrapping paper and took it to the garbage can out back already.

Joy, Rini and Meika were headed back to Houston and Asia and Butchie were back at their house laden down with all their baby gifts. Pain, Goon and Bruise never returned after Blue and his boys showed up, so it was safe to assume they were patrolling the grounds looking for Man.

"Probably down to the lake or just laying low to give us time alone, knowing Tay's meddling ass. I should have known something was up with you, she encouraged me to give you a chance over and over again, usually she's not like that," Yolan remarked and moved into the great room to take down all the decorations.

"I got it, are we trashing this stuff, or should we save it for later?" he asked, completely ignoring her comment and looking over at her pointedly with a smirk.

"I was going to just take them down and let Tay and Asia decide what they want to do with them," she answered, her eyes narrowed, *here we go*, she thought.

"I know you said we would talk at your house but I got to know, why? Why didn't you tell me the minute you found out?" Ryan asked, pulling down a picture of a stork with a baby.

"Honestly, I was going to tell you that day I called you, but after the way you shut me down– I decided to wait until I was back in Houston. I know I should have at least tried again to reach you but I've been on autopilot, trying to get my life back to as close to normal as I can. And after all I said to you and you said to me, I was afraid of your reaction and what you would say about it," Yolan admitted, placing the last of the decorations on the table and reaching over to turn off the lights, leaving them in the dark. Alternating tiles in the floor began to glow, lighting their way to the kitchen and backdoor.

"That is so damn tight! Leave it to my cousin to have some futuristic shit in his house to keep from running into shit!" Ryan remarked, looking down at the softly lit floor.

"Yeah, he wanted to make sure Tay could find her way around safely in the dark, especially since she can't see her feet anymore. They are all over their house in Houston too. They are motion activated too, so yeah, pretty cool," Yolan explained, walking back through the kitchen and opening the back door, she waited until he was standing next to her on the back steps and closed and locked the door behind them.

"Do you have keys to their house in Houston too?" Ryan asked, after falling in step next to her as they walked back over to her house.

"Yes, but of course you knew that already because so do you, right, Ryan?" she asked, pushing the key in her front pocket.

"Correct, as does the security team, just in case," he said quietly, taking her own house keys from her hand and opening the back door to her house.

The scent of heavy-duty cleaning supplies hit her nose and sent her rushing to the downstairs washroom where her stomach turned inside out.

"Are you going to be okay in here tonight?" he asked in concern when she wandered into the living room a few minutes later, dabbing her mouth with a wet towel after brushing her teeth. He was in the kitchen pouring himself something to drink.

"Make yourself at home I guess," she mumbled as she sat down on the couch. She noticed he had opened all the doors and windows, a breeze was lifting the filmy curtains in the living room as it blew through.

The smell was still there but not so strong. "I should be fine. It was just really strong because the house was closed up when we first got here," she answered as he walked back into the room.

He set a glass of ginger ale in front of her as he sipped on a glass of ice water. "Good, just let me know if we need to go over to one of the other houses or the main house," Ryan said, making a point not to sit next to her but across from her.

"Thank you and I'm fine, Ryan," she said, a little snappier than she intended too.

"Over at the house you said you didn't know how I'd react to you being pregnant, or what I would say, so because of that you decided not to tell me at all?" he asked, putting his glass on a coaster, leaning forward looking at his hands clasped in front of him.

The look he gave her made her stomach lurch again, so she quickly took a few sips of ginger ale. "No, of course not, Ryan. I'm a bitch but not a fucking bitch, geez! I just wanted to wait until the dust settled and we were all back in Houston before I brought it up," she explained, already feeling defensive and annoyed.

She prayed he would accept her explanation and move on, she didn't want to go any deeper into the recesses of her mind and memories.

"Why though? Regardless of what was and is going on

and where you are or were, you are pregnant with my baby," and I had the right to know," Ryan emphasized looking over at her, studying her face.

Yolan screamed on the inside, she should have known he was going to pick apart everything she said.

"Because of how things were left between us, and because I was afraid to face you, honestly. Besides, I didn't want your feelings for me to cloud your judgement when it came to the pregnancy," Yolan explained and took another sip of ginger ale hugging one of the throw pillows in front of her as Ryan quietly processed her words and scanned her face.

"Hmph, cloud my judgement? Wow, Yo that's deep. What did you think I was going to do besides ask you how you felt about all of this, and have a civilized conversation about where we go from here?" Ryan asked her quietly, shaking his head sadly, his expression full of hurt and annoyance

Yolan broke their eye contact and looked up at the ceiling as tears she didn't want to shed slipped from her eyes anyway. "Ryan, it's just that I-I want to keep this baby and I wasn't sure you would feel the same way, especially after all of my crazy, and your place being shot up, and well, just everything," Yolan admitted looking over at him briefly through her tears before she had to look away again.

His face was set, expressionless, as he ran his finger down the condensation on his glass of ice water as he studied her. "Let me guess, you've been pregnant before and the father made you terminate the pregnancy?" he asked, still studying her, Yolan closed her eyes briefly before making herself look over at him.

"No, he just constantly reminded me that if I did ever end up pregnant, he wanted it terminated immediately, it was not up for discussion, said he didn't want kids, ever. Being curious, as well as a glutton for punishment, I had Joy run a check on him a few years back, and not only is he married, he has three kids. It wasn't that he didn't want kids, he didn't want kids with someone like me." She bit her trembling lip to keep from crying out in frustration.

She knew how fucked up she was because of Deon, and she hated it, she wished there was a switch in her body she could flip and turn off all these feelings but there was no quick fix for her type of hurt.

"Someone like you? What does that even mean, Yolan? I wish you could see what I see, what I'm sure everyone sees when they look at you. You are a phenomenal woman. You're strong, successful, and so fucking beautiful it can be heart-stopping to look at you sometimes. If this is about what your line of work encompasses then remember this, I had no idea who the fuck you were until Jazz told me. I honestly thought you were once in a seriously bad, abusive relationship and got out and that's why you carried a gun," he informed her before taking a healthy drink of ice water. "Let me ask you this, if your reluctance to be with me was about your line of work then why didn't you step down and be like Asia, in the crew but not *in* the crew?" Ryan asked, messing with his glass again, water dropped from his fingertip as his eyes stayed on her face.

"Not you, too! Why does everyone think I want to step down? I realized something in the last two months, I love my job, and more importantly, I love my crew and I know I am fucking great at what I do, so why would I want to do anything else? Those ladies and Jazz and the rest of the team are my family, and I would fight to the death for any of them, and I am not and will never be ashamed of that, or my line of business ever again.

"I spent so much of my life trying to belong, and being constantly reminded of why I didn't because of who my family was, that by the time I was old enough to know that those opinions aren't the ones that matter, I had already had years of practice building walls. And when I finally let my guard down, I got my heart ripped out of my chest and never really got over it," she admitted, looking down at her manicured toes, soon she wouldn't be able to see them.

"Who hurt you, Yolan? Please tell me his name so I can make him disappear. Is that what it will take for you to finally let go and stop punishing me for his narrow-minded mistakes?" Ryan asked with a pained impatient look on his face. "I know what I texted you when you called, but it doesn't matter because, in case you haven't noticed, I'm in love you, Yolan. The thought of my seed growing inside of you makes me so fucking happy I could burst, but I can't keep competing with a ghost and insecurities of your past, I just can't do it, Yolan. I'm sorry.

We will figure out together what we need to do to be the best parents we can be for our child but for the time being, to protect myself from anymore heartache and pain, I have to let you go. Give you the time you need to heal and to stop avoiding the pain from the past you never dealt with." Ryan's eyes clouded with tears, he pinched the bridge of his nose to keep them from falling as he picked up his glass and drank all of his water.

Yolan closed her eyes and nodded, tears continued to fall freely down her face. "I understand and thank you, Ryan for fighting as hard as you did. No one has ever made me feel as special as you did, but you're right, I have a lot of healing to do before I can give you, or honestly everyone in my life, the genuine love they truly deserve," Yolan admitted using the towel she had walked into the living room with to wipe her tears away. She felt relieved and devastated at the same time.

It took her all of this time, but now she knew way down deep in her heart of hearts that Ryan was *nothing* like Deon, but she was still so afraid to let herself love him. Until she could give him her heart as freely as he gave his, there was no reason for them to be together including the baby growing inside of her.

"Needless to say, who knows what the future will bring? I have no plans of being with anyone else and I will be with you every step of the way through this pregnancy, so we will see what we see, Ny." He stood up and reached out to take her hand bringing her to her feet too.

She allowed him to pull her close and wrap his arms around her, rocking her in his embrace as she cried into the front of his shirt.

Epilogue

Five months later

Yolan stood out on the back patio of the beach house in Barbados, looking out at the waves quietly hitting the shore. She smiled with her hand over her belly as laughter from her entire family swelled from inside the house. She and the entire crew were relaxing and taking some much deserved time off.

Both Asia and Tayana had given birth to healthy babies, Asia and Butchie had their little princess, Anisa, Jazz and Tayana had their little prince they named Jihad since he came into this world in the middle of a war. Man was still on the run but so far nowhere to be found, one thing was for sure he had left Houston and the hunt continued. No one would truly relax until they were 100% sure he was gone for good.

Asia and Butchie left Plano shortly after hearing Man was no longer in Houston to have Anisa at home surrounded by her family. True to her word, when they moved back Yolan did too, she was now living in one of the suites in the building Ryan had purchased.

She planned to stay there until Man was caught, then and only then would she go back to her house. She spent half of her free time on the rooftop of her building either in the greenhouse or visiting her 'boyfriend' the koi who seemed to take a liking to her from the first time she sat on the wall beneath the waterfall, she called him Keith. The other half of her free time were her self-care days, she went on walks, visited museums, and went to her therapy appointments.

They still only used the brick-and-mortar office three times a week to be safe and that was usually when they had meetings and showings scheduled. Security detail followed them all wherever they went.

Ryan went to every prenatal appointment, ultrasound and Lamaze class she had. At first it was hard to be around him and not throw her arms around his waist and kiss him the way she wanted to but she promised him and more importantly herself she would not even attempt to blur those lines until she was really ready to.

"Hey, you want to hold your godson before I put him to bed? I know you're about to go down and walk on the beach and you won't get back until after he's asleep," Tayana asked, Jihad was cradled in her arms looking up at his mother, his eyelids growing heavy.

"You know I do, give me my little guy," Yolan said, her face spreading into a full thousand-watt smile as Tayana placed the baby gently in her arms.

Yolan rocked him back and forth studying his handsome face, he was a perfect blend of Jazz and Tayana with Jazz's light eyes and his mother's temper. "Tay, you know this boy is going to be a heartbreaker, right? Remember how he had all the nurses swooning?" Yolan asked looking over at Tayana, who rolled her eyes and reached out to take him back as soon as his eyes finally closed and stayed closed. He loved being in his Auntie Yo's arms, Anisa was the same way.

"He's only three months old, Yo! Can't he at least learn to hold his own bottle before you got him chasing loose women? Damn! Come on, Jihad let's put you to bed and get you away from your crazy ass auntie and her foolishness," Tayana said softly, smiling down at her son.

"Whatever, Tay, I never said he would be chasing them but we already know they will be chasing him. Good night, Jihad, Auntie Yo loves you and I got your back!" she whispered, kissing him on the forehead before Tayana turned to take him back inside and put him to bed.

"We love you too, Yo. Enjoy your walk and be careful, don't get too close to the water, you fuck around and hurt my babies I'm going to have to kick your ass!" Tayana threatened as Yolan started to walk down the stairs that led to the beach and her favorite spot on the rocks near the water.

She had a favorite rock she liked to watch the sunset from, sometimes when the water was choppy, waves would reach her rock and wet her pants or the hem of her dress. Tayana was worried that one day a wave big enough could hit the rock and take her under.

It still tripped her out when she thought about it, she wasn't just having one baby, she was having two. Two little perfect blends of her and Ryan, the best parts of both of them were growing inside of her and would be in her arms in a few months.

She sighed contently as she watched the sunset, she always listened for the sizzling sound as the last light of the sun disappeared into the sea, oddly enough for the first time ever she heard it. Or at least she thought she did until she looked over her shoulder and right into the honey brown eyes of her children's father, Ryan Devoe.

"What are you doing out here? I thought you couldn't come, you said you had important business to attend to," Yolan asked with surprise, still looking over her shoulder at him. He was still so damn handsome and never ceased to take her breath away.

He moved closer to 'her' rock and leaned his back against it as he looked out at the water. He had that beach bum look, khaki shorts, button down shirt on but unbuttoned and sandals in his hands.

"I did, but as I sat there in my third meeting not even remembering what the first two had been about, I knew it was time to leave." He reached down and picked up a seashell and started rubbing the sand off still staring out at the ocean.

"That's not normal for you, what had you or has you so distracted?" Yolan asked, stretching her legs out in front of her and crossing her ankles looking over at him. She wanted to reach her hand and touch his back, drop kisses on his shoulders but turned her head to clear her racy thoughts from her mind.

"A beautiful woman. I was so busy thinking about her I couldn't concentrate," Ryan admitted, finally looking over at her again.

"Oh, my fucking God, No!" Yolan screamed inside her head, it was loud enough to shatter glass! Her and her insecurities had cost her the only man she would ever truly love! Yolan hated the wench already and would forever because if she was distracting him already, then she had already wiggled her way inside his heart, where she used to be!

Despite how she felt, she forced a smile on her face and looked over at him. "Well, she must really be something special to be able to distract you like that already. I'm happy for you," she lied, blinking rapidly, praying it was dark enough to mask her teary eyes.

"She is, and I'm glad she is starting to realize it, too. I'm going to ask her to marry me," Ryan said, looking down at his feet, moving the sand around with his toes.

"Uh, what?" Yolan asked him, her heartbeat was echoing

in her ears as she retasted her dinner. Marry her? He barely knew this heffa and he's going to marry her? She hadn't even had the babies yet and they already have a stepmama! What the hell was he thinking? She felt her face get hot as jealousy and anger fought it out in her body.

"I'm going to ask her to marry me. I can't imagine my life without her in it so I'm going to lock her down before someone else does," he declared, pulling a ring box out of his pocket.

Yolan looked at the beautiful yellow diamond and white gold ring and snapped, "Ryan are you fucking kidding me? You're going to propose to a female you've only known for a hot minute to keep the next man from scooping her up? Are you out of your damn mind!" Yolan yelled, glaring over at him, looking at him like he was crazy.

"I know, but I love her, Ny. I want her to be mine and only mine. I want her to know no matter what someone said or tried to do to break her down that I love every part of her and wouldn't trade her for anything in the world. She is my world, Ny and I need her to know that. Do you think she'll have me? Do you think she can love me? I don't care if it's a fraction of the love I feel for her, her love is all I want and need," Ryan said and pulled the ring out of the box and slid it on the third finger of her left hand, a perfect fit.

"Seriously, Ryan! Why would you buy her a ring and put it on my finger? That is so not cool!" Yolan said, still seething, her mind going between cussing him out and demanding this female's name so she could make sure The Firm ran a check on her and so she could have a little talk with her.

"Damn, pregnancy brain ain't no joke, you are slow as hell, woman! The ring fits because I'm talking about you, Nyiesha! In those meetings all I could think about was you walking around on this beach in sundresses and bathing suits, your sun-kissed, soft skin glowing. Then I started thinking about how bad I wanted to see you and not just for an appointment or class, either. But to see you, to hold you and spend time with you, to make love to you again," he told her looking at her with mischief dancing in his eyes. "I know what I said in Plano, but I love you, Nyiesha Marinna Yolan Belle and you and these babies are everything to me, so enough of this separation bullshit, will you marry me?" Ryan asked and took both of her hands in his and kissed them both softly. His honey brown eyes locked with hers even in the darkness on the beach, as he waited patiently for her answer.

Yolan looked from the ring to him and back again until her vision was blurry. She asked herself, was she ready? Could she give 100% percent of herself to Ryan and leave the past behind her once and for all?

She realized in that moment she could and for the first time since that heartbreak, she felt so free. The happiness that was slow in building, welled up inside of her as she began to nod before shouting at the top of her lungs.

"Yes! Yes! I will marry you and I love you too, Ryan Devoe!"

Ryan scooped her up in his arms and held her tight, kissing her all over her face before carefully putting her back down on her rock and sitting down next to her.

"You have no idea how happy you just made me. I know you are still working through those demons from the past, but we can work on them together, baby. Hell, I will even go to therapy with you if you need me to," Ryan vowed, pulling her into his arms and bringing his mouth to meet hers.

Shivers shot through her body as his lips touched hers for the first time in over seven months. Happy tears poured from her eyes as he pulled his lips away from her and looked down at her, the look of love mixed with desire made her glow.

"Ryan, I'm sorry for putting you through so much when all you have ever wanted to do was make me happy. I was so caught up in keeping things from you I didn't see all the things you were sharing with me," she admitted, looking at him sheepishly. "You're right, I still have some work to do on myself but I thank God you're willing to be by my side while I do it. You don't have to come to therapy with me though, that's not what I need from you," Yolan said, allowing him to reposition her until she was sitting between his legs on the rock with her back against his chest looking out at the ocean.

"Well, then exactly what do you need from me, Ny?" he asked, kissing her softly on the forehead.

"For you to keep on doing what you've been doing since the day you met me," Yolan answered, loving how it felt to be in his arms again.

"And what's that?" he asked softly, kissing her around the ear, making her tingle all over.

"Keep seeing me, seeing who I really am, and loving me anyway." she sighed constantly as his lips traveled from her ear and dropped down the length of her neck.

With Ryan's love and support, she knew no matter how long it took to erase the ghosts from the past, she would be just fine.

"Did he just do what I think he did? Did he just propose?" Tayana asked Jazz, dancing excitedly, watching Ryan and Yolan out on the beach from their balcony.

Jazz dropped a soft kiss on Jihad's head as he walked over to join Tayana on the balcony. He slipped his arms around her waist and pulled her close.

"I believe that's exactly what he did, my cousin is a lot like me, he sees something he likes and goes after it. No matter how difficult getting it might be," he whispered, kissing Tayana softly on the lips.

She put her arms around his neck and went to close her eyes when sudden movement by the pier caught her eye. Jazz felt her tense up and immediately followed her line of sight, a man was running up the beach towards Ryan and Yolan, gun drawn.

He was less than three feet away as Tayana started to scream Yolan's name to warn them. A shot rang out and he quickly crumpled on the sand in mid-stride. She saw Joy and Meika jump over the wooden railing and race down the beach to him to make sure he was dead. Goon and Pain came running from the opposite direction.

Ryan and Yolan sprang apart and were quickly on their feet, each with a gun in their hands.

Two seconds later Tayana's phone rang. "Whisper, sound the alarm and let's move everyone now! That man who Joy just shot was Kisho, your brother Calvin's business partner and you know if he's over here then Calvin brought him, and they didn't come alone. I don't know what the fuck Man told Calvin to make him come back stateside, but we need to find out and find out fast. Calvin is a high roller in Japan and those are problems we just don't need right now or ever!" Meika informed her quickly then hanging up.

Jazz already had Jihad strapped in his car seat and was pulling on his shoes, his 357 was holstered at his side. Tayana pulled on a pair of jeans and tucked Mary Jane in the back of her pants. "Shit, until now I forgot the first rule of war my Daddy taught us. *Stand up against family be prepared to fall at the family's hand.* I guess it's time my brothers learn what that really means. It's time to stop simply moving pieces around and knock these piss boys clean off my muthafuckin' board!

Joy Bussu

Blessings! I am 48-year-old Joy Bussu. Eighteen years married, mother of four, grandmother of one. I was born in Wichita Falls, Texas, but raised in Denver, Colorado, where I currently reside with my beautiful family.

I have always had a love for the written word. I devoured books from the time I could string sentences together and I have always loved to write. Once I gave birth to my youngest child and only daughter, I was finally ready to attempt to write my first book. It took me over ten years to complete it.

Holding the first copy of my self-published book was the opening of the flood gate I never even realized I was holding back. Writing is my passion and my life and it is my pleasure and deepest honor to be able to share it with the world. My dream is to touch as many as humanly possible with my work.

Visit my webpage

Don't miss these exciting titles by Joy Bussu and Blushing Books!

Dangerous Love series
The Art of Love
Love Don't Live Here Anymore

Nieko's Treasure
Whispers
Makia's Bodyguard

Anthologies
12 Naughty Days of Christmas 2020

Blushing Books

Blushing Books is the oldest eBook publisher on the web. We've been running websites that publish steamy romance and erotica since 1999, and we have been selling eBooks since 2003. We have free and promotional offerings that change weekly, so please do visit us at http://www.blushingbooks.com/free.

Blushing Books Newsletter

Please join the Blushing Books newsletter
to receive updates & special promotional offers.
You can also join by using your mobile phone:
Just text **BLUSHING** to 22828.

Every month, one new sign up via text messaging will receive
a $25.00 Amazon gift card, so sign up today!